The Eight Strokes of the Clock

The Eight Strokes of the Clock

Maurice Leblanc

MINT EDITIONS

The Eight Strokes of the Clock was first published in 1922.

This edition published by Mint Editions 2021.

ISBN 9781513292427 | E-ISBN 9781513295275

Published by Mint Editions®

MINT
EDITIONS

minteditionbooks.com

Publishing Director: Jennifer Newens
Design & Production: Rachel Lopez Metzger
Project Manager: Micaela Clark
Typesetting: Westchester Publishing Services

Contents

Author's Note   7

I. On the Top of the Tower   9

II. The Water-Bottle   30

III. The Case of Jean Louis   51

IV. The Tell-Tale Film   70

V. Thérèse and Germaine   90

VI. The Lady with the Hatchet   110

VII. Footprints in the Snow   129

VIII. At the Sign of Mercury   152

CONTENTS

Author's Note

These adventures were told to me in the old days by Arsène Lupin, as though they had happened to a friend of his, named Prince Rénine. As for me, considering the way in which they were conducted, the actions, the behaviour and the very character of the hero, I find it very difficult not to identify the two friends as one and the same person. Arsène Lupin is gifted with a powerful imagination and is quite capable of attributing to himself adventures which are not his at all and of disowning those which are really his. The reader will judge for himself.

M. L.

I

On the Top of the Tower

H ortense Daniel pushed her window ajar and whispered:

"Are you there, Rossigny?"

"I am here," replied a voice from the shrubbery at the front of the house.

Leaning forward, she saw a rather fat man looking up at her out of a gross red face with its cheeks and chin set in unpleasantly fair whiskers.

"Well?" he asked.

"Well, I had a great argument with my uncle and aunt last night. They absolutely refuse to sign the document of which my lawyer sent them the draft, or to restore the dowry squandered by my husband."

"But your uncle is responsible by the terms of the marriage-settlement."

"No matter. He refuses."

"Well, what do you propose to do?"

"Are you still determined to run away with me?" she asked, with a laugh.

"More so than ever."

"Your intentions are strictly honourable, remember!"

"Just as you please. You know that I am madly in love with you."

"Unfortunately I am not madly in love with you!"

"Then what made you choose me?"

"Chance. I was bored. I was growing tired of my humdrum existence. So I'm ready to run risks. . . Here's my luggage: catch!"

She let down from the window a couple of large leather kit-bags. Rossigny caught them in his arms.

"The die is cast," she whispered. "Go and wait for me with your car at the If cross-roads. I shall come on horseback."

"Hang it, I can't run off with your horse!"

"He will go home by himself."

"Capital! . . . Oh, by the way. . ."

"What is it?"

"Who is this Prince Rénine, who's been here the last three days and whom nobody seems to know?"

"I don't know much about him. My uncle met him at a friend's shoot and asked him here to stay."

"You seem to have made a great impression on him. You went for a long ride with him yesterday. He's a man I don't care for."

"In two hours I shall have left the house in your company. The scandal will cool him off. . . Well, we've talked long enough. We have no time to lose."

For a few minutes she stood watching the fat man bending under the weight of her traps as he moved away in the shelter of an empty avenue. Then she closed the window.

Outside, in the park, the huntsmen's horns were sounding the reveille. The hounds burst into frantic baying. It was the opening day of the hunt that morning at the Château de la Marèze, where, every year, in the first week in September, the Comte d'Aigleroche, a mighty hunter before the Lord, and his countess were accustomed to invite a few personal friends and the neighbouring landowners.

Hortense slowly finished dressing, put on a riding-habit, which revealed the lines of her supple figure, and a wide-brimmed felt hat, which encircled her lovely face and auburn hair, and sat down to her writing-desk, at which she wrote to her uncle, M. d'Aigleroche, a farewell letter to be delivered to him that evening. It was a difficult letter to word; and, after beginning it several times, she ended by giving up the idea.

"I will write to him later," she said to herself, "when his anger has cooled down."

And she went downstairs to the dining-room.

Enormous logs were blazing in the hearth of the lofty room. The walls were hung with trophies of rifles and shotguns. The guests were flocking in from every side, shaking hands with the Comte d'Aigleroche, one of those typical country squires, heavily and powerfully built, who lives only for hunting and shooting. He was standing before the fire, with a large glass of old brandy in his hand, drinking the health of each new arrival.

Hortense kissed him absently:

"What, uncle! You who are usually so sober!"

"Pooh!" he said. "A man may surely indulge himself a little once a year! . . ."

"Aunt will give you a scolding!"

"Your aunt has one of her sick headaches and is not coming down. Besides," he added, gruffly, "it is not her business. . . and still less is it yours, my dear child."

Prince Rénine came up to Hortense. He was a young man, very smartly dressed, with a narrow and rather pale face, whose eyes held by turns the gentlest and the harshest, the most friendly and the most satirical expression. He bowed to her, kissed her hand and said:

"May I remind you of your kind promise, dear madame?"

"My promise?"

"Yes, we agreed that we should repeat our delightful excursion of yesterday and try to go over that old boarded-up place the look of which made us so curious. It seems to be known as the Domaine de Halingre."

She answered a little curtly:

"I'm extremely sorry, monsieur, but it would be rather far and I'm feeling a little done up. I shall go for a canter in the park and come indoors again."

There was a pause. Then Serge Rénine said, smiling, with his eyes fixed on hers and in a voice which she alone could hear:

"I am sure that you'll keep your promise and that you'll let me come with you. It would be better."

"For whom? For you, you mean?"

"For you, too, I assure you."

She coloured slightly, but did not reply, shook hands with a few people around her and left the room.

A groom was holding the horse at the foot of the steps. She mounted and set off towards the woods beyond the park.

It was a cool, still morning. Through the leaves, which barely quivered, the sky showed crystalline blue. Hortense rode at a walk down winding avenues which in half an hour brought her to a country-side of ravines and bluffs intersected by the high-road.

She stopped. There was not a sound. Rossigny must have stopped his engine and concealed the car in the thickets around the If cross-roads.

She was five hundred yards at most from that circular space. After hesitating for a few seconds, she dismounted, tied her horse carelessly, so that he could release himself by the least effort and return to the house, shrouded her face in the long brown veil that hung over her shoulders and walked on.

As she expected, she saw Rossigny directly she reached the first turn in the road. He ran up to her and drew her into the coppice!

"Quick, quick! Oh, I was so afraid that you would be late. . . or even change your mind! And here you are! It seems too good to be true!"

She smiled:

"You appear to be quite happy to do an idiotic thing!"

"I should think I *am* happy! And so will you be, I swear you will! Your life will be one long fairy-tale. You shall have every luxury, and all the money you can wish for."

"I want neither money nor luxuries."

"What then?"

"Happiness."

"You can safely leave your happiness to me."

She replied, jestingly:

"I rather doubt the quality of the happiness which you would give me."

"Wait! You'll see! You'll see!"

They had reached the motor. Rossigny, still stammering expressions of delight, started the engine. Hortense stepped in and wrapped herself in a wide cloak. The car followed the narrow, grassy path which led back to the cross-roads and Rossigny was accelerating the speed, when he was suddenly forced to pull up. A shot had rung out from the neighbouring wood, on the right. The car was swerving from side to side.

"A front tire burst," shouted Rossigny, leaping to the ground.

"Not a bit of it!" cried Hortense. "Somebody fired!"

"Impossible, my dear! Don't be so absurd!"

At that moment, two slight shocks were felt and two more reports were heard, one after the other, some way off and still in the wood.

Rossigny snarled:

"The back tires burst now. . . both of them. . . But who, in the devil's name, can the ruffian be? . . . Just let me get hold of him, that's all! . . ."

He clambered up the road-side slope. There was no one there. Moreover, the leaves of the coppice blocked the view.

"Damn it! Damn it!" he swore. "You were right: somebody was firing at the car! Oh, this is a bit thick! We shall be held up for hours! Three tires to mend! . . . But what are you doing, dear girl?"

Hortense herself had alighted from the car. She ran to him, greatly excited:

"I'm going."

"But why?"

"I want to know. Some one fired. I want to know who it was."

"Don't let us separate, please!"

"Do you think I'm going to wait here for you for hours?"

"What about your running away? . . . All our plans. . . ?"

"We'll discuss that to-morrow. Go back to the house. Take back my things with you. . . And good-bye for the present."

She hurried, left him, had the good luck to find her horse and set off at a gallop in a direction leading away from La Marèze.

There was not the least doubt in her mind that the three shots had been fired by Prince Rénine.

"It was he," she muttered, angrily, "it was he. No one else would be capable of such behaviour."

Besides, he had warned her, in his smiling, masterful way, that he would expect her.

She was weeping with rage and humiliation. At that moment, had she found herself face to face with Prince Rénine, she could have struck him with her riding-whip.

Before her was the rugged and picturesque stretch of country which lies between the Orne and the Sarthe, above Alençon, and which is known as Little Switzerland. Steep hills compelled her frequently to moderate her pace, the more so as she had to cover some six miles before reaching her destination. But, though the speed at which she rode became less headlong, though her physical effort gradually slackened, she nevertheless persisted in her indignation against Prince Rénine. She bore him a grudge not only for the unspeakable action of which he had been guilty, but also for his behaviour to her during the last three days, his persistent attentions, his assurance, his air of excessive politeness.

She was nearly there. In the bottom of a valley, an old park-wall, full of cracks and covered with moss and weeds, revealed the ball-turret of a château and a few windows with closed shutters. This was the Domaine de Halingre.

She followed the wall and turned a corner. In the middle of the crescent-shaped space before which lay the entrance-gates, Serge Rénine stood waiting beside his horse.

She sprang to the ground, and, as he stepped forward, hat in hand, thanking her for coming, she cried:

"One word, monsieur, to begin with. Something quite inexplicable happened just now. Three shots were fired at a motor-car in which I was sitting. Did you fire those shots?"

"Yes."

She seemed dumbfounded:

"Then you confess it?"

"You have asked a question, madame, and I have answered it."

"But how dared you? What gave you the right?"

"I was not exercising a right, madame; I was performing a duty!"

"Indeed! And what duty, pray?"

"The duty of protecting you against a man who is trying to profit by your troubles."

"I forbid you to speak like that. I am responsible for my own actions, and I decided upon them in perfect liberty."

"Madame, I overheard your conversation with M. Rossigny this morning and it did not appear to me that you were accompanying him with a light heart. I admit the ruthlessness and bad taste of my interference and I apologise for it humbly; but I risked being taken for a ruffian in order to give you a few hours for reflection."

"I have reflected fully, monsieur. When I have once made up my mind to a thing, I do not change it."

"Yes, madame, you do, sometimes. If not, why are you here instead of there?"

Hortense was confused for a moment. All her anger had subsided. She looked at Rénine with the surprise which one experiences when confronted with certain persons who are unlike their fellows, more capable of performing unusual actions, more generous and disinterested. She realised perfectly that he was acting without any ulterior motive or calculation, that he was, as he had said, merely fulfilling his duty as a gentleman to a woman who has taken the wrong turning.

Speaking very gently, he said:

"I know very little about you, madame, but enough to make me wish to be of use to you. You are twenty-six years old and have lost both your parents. Seven years ago, you became the wife of the Comte d'Aigleroche's nephew by marriage, who proved to be of unsound mind, half insane indeed, and had to be confined. This made it impossible for you to obtain a divorce and compelled you, since your dowry had been squandered, to live with your uncle and at his expense. It's a depressing environment. The count and countess do not agree. Years ago, the count was deserted by his first wife, who ran away with the countess' first husband. The abandoned husband and wife decided out of spite to unite their fortunes, but found nothing but disappointment and ill-will in this second marriage. And you suffer the consequences. They lead a monotonous, narrow, lonely life for eleven months or more out of the year. One day, you met M. Rossigny, who fell in love with you and suggested an elopement. You did not care for him. But you were bored, your youth was being wasted, you longed for the unexpected, for adventure. . . in a word, you accepted with the very definite intention of keeping your admirer at arm's length, but also with the rather ingenuous hope that the scandal would force your uncle's hand and make him account for his trusteeship and assure you of an independent existence. That is how you stand. At present you have to choose between placing yourself in M. Rossigny's hands. . . or trusting yourself to me."

She raised her eyes to his. What did he mean? What was the purport of this offer which he made so seriously, like a friend who asks nothing but to prove his devotion?

After a moment's silence, he took the two horses by the bridle and tied them up. Then he examined the heavy gates, each of which was strengthened by two planks nailed cross-wise. An electoral poster, dated twenty years earlier, showed that no one had entered the domain since that time.

Rénine tore up one of the iron posts which supported a railing that ran round the crescent and used it as a lever. The rotten planks gave way. One of them uncovered the lock, which he attacked with a big knife, containing a number of blades and implements. A minute later, the gate opened on a waste of bracken which led up to a long, dilapidated building, with a turret at each corner and a sort of a belvedere, built on a taller tower, in the middle.

The Prince turned to Hortense:

"You are in no hurry," he said. "You will form your decision this evening; and, if M. Rossigny succeeds in persuading you for the second time, I give you my word of honour that I shall not cross your path. Until then, grant me the privilege of your company. We made up our minds yesterday to inspect the château. Let us do so. Will you? It is as good a way as any of passing the time and I have a notion that it will not be uninteresting."

He had a way of talking which compelled obedience. He seemed to be commanding and entreating at the same time. Hortense did not even seek to shake off the enervation into which her will was slowly sinking. She followed him to a half-demolished flight of steps at the top of which was a door likewise strengthened by planks nailed in the form of a cross.

Rénine went to work in the same way as before. They entered a spacious hall paved with white and black flagstones, furnished with old sideboards and choir-stalls and adorned with a carved escutcheon which displayed the remains of armorial bearings, representing an eagle standing on a block of stone, all half-hidden behind a veil of cobwebs which hung down over a pair of folding-doors.

"The door of the drawing-room, evidently," said Rénine.

He found this more difficult to open; and it was only by repeatedly charging it with his shoulder that he was able to move one of the doors.

Hortense had not spoken a word. She watched not without surprise this series of forcible entries, which were accomplished with a really masterly skill. He guessed her thoughts and, turning round, said in a serious voice:

"It's child's-play to me. I was a locksmith once."

She seized his arm and whispered:

"Listen!"

"To what?" he asked.

She increased the pressure of her hand, to demand silence. The next moment, he murmured:

"It's really very strange."

"Listen, listen!" Hortense repeated, in bewilderment. "Can it be possible?"

They heard, not far from where they were standing, a sharp sound, the sound of a light tap recurring at regular intervals; and they had only to listen attentively to recognise the ticking of a clock. Yes, it was this and nothing else that broke the profound silence of the dark room; it was indeed the deliberate ticking, rhythmical as the beat of a metronome, produced by a heavy brass pendulum. That was it! And nothing could be more impressive than the measured pulsation of this trivial mechanism, which by some miracle, some inexplicable phenomenon, had continued to live in the heart of the dead château.

"And yet," stammered Hortense, without daring to raise her voice, "no one has entered the house?"

"No one."

"And it is quite impossible for that clock to have kept going for twenty years without being wound up?"

"Quite impossible."

"Then. . . ?"

Serge Rénine opened the three windows and threw back the shutters.

He and Hortense were in a drawing-room, as he had thought; and the room showed not the least sign of disorder. The chairs were in their places. Not a piece of furniture was missing. The people who had lived there and who had made it the most individual room in their house had gone away leaving everything just as it was, the books which they used to read, the knick-knacks on the tables and consoles.

Rénine examined the old grandfather's clock, contained in its tall carved case which showed the disk of the pendulum through an oval pane of glass. He opened the door of the clock. The weights hanging from the cords were at their lowest point.

At that moment there was a click. The clock struck eight with a serious note which Hortense was never to forget.

"How extraordinary!" she said.

"Extraordinary indeed," said he, "for the works are exceedingly simple and would hardly keep going for a week."

"And do you see nothing out of the common?"

"No, nothing. . . or, at least. . ."

He stooped and, from the back of the case, drew a metal tube which was concealed by the weights. Holding it up to the light:

"A telescope," he said, thoughtfully. "Why did they hide it? . . . And they left it drawn out to its full length. . . That's odd. . . What does it mean?"

The clock, as is sometimes usual, began to strike a second time, sounding eight strokes. Rénine closed the case and continued his inspection without putting his telescope down. A wide arch led from the drawing-room to a smaller apartment, a sort of smoking-room. This also was furnished, but contained a glass case for guns of which the rack was empty. Hanging on a panel near by was a calendar with the date of the 5th of September.

"Oh," cried Hortense, in astonishment, "the same date as to-day! . . . They tore off the leaves until the 5th of September. . . And this is the anniversary! What an astonishing coincidence!"

"Astonishing," he echoed. "It's the anniversary of their departure. . . twenty years ago to-day."

"You must admit," she said, "that all this is incomprehensible.

"Yes, of course. . . but, all the same. . . perhaps not."

"Have you any idea?"

He waited a few seconds before replying:

"What puzzles me is this telescope hidden, dropped in that corner, at the last moment. I wonder what it was used for. . . From the ground-floor windows you see nothing but the trees in the garden. . . and the same, I expect, from all the windows. . . We are in a valley, without the least open horizon. . . To use the telescope, one would have to go up to the top of the house. . . Shall we go up?"

She did not hesitate. The mystery surrounding the whole adventure excited her curiosity so keenly that she could think of nothing but accompanying Rénine and assisting him in his investigations.

They went upstairs accordingly, and, on the second floor, came to a landing where they found the spiral staircase leading to the belvedere.

At the top of this was a platform in the open air, but surrounded by a parapet over six feet high.

"There must have been battlements which have been filled in since," observed Prince Rénine. "Look here, there were loop-holes at one time. They may have been blocked."

"In any case," she said, "the telescope was of no use up here either and we may as well go down again."

"I don't agree," he said. "Logic tells us that there must have been some gap through which the country could be seen and this was the spot where the telescope was used."

He hoisted himself by his wrists to the top of the parapet and then saw that this point of vantage commanded the whole of the valley, including the park, with its tall trees marking the horizon; and, beyond, a depression in a wood surmounting a hill, at a distance of some seven or eight hundred yards, stood another tower, squat and in ruins, covered with ivy from top to bottom.

Rénine resumed his inspection. He seemed to consider that the key to the problem lay in the use to which the telescope was put and that the problem would be solved if only they could discover this use.

He studied the loop-holes one after the other. One of them, or rather the place which it had occupied, attracted his attention above the rest. In the middle of the layer of plaster, which had served to block it, there was a hollow filled with earth in which plants had grown. He pulled out the plants and removed the earth, thus clearing the mouth of a hole some five inches in diameter, which completely penetrated the wall. On bending forward, Rénine perceived that this deep and narrow opening inevitably carried the eye, above the dense tops of the trees and through the depression in the hill, to the ivy-clad tower.

At the bottom of this channel, in a sort of groove which ran through it like a gutter, the telescope fitted so exactly that it was quite impossible to shift it, however little, either to the right or to the left.

Rénine, after wiping the outside of the lenses, while taking care not to disturb the lie of the instrument by a hair's breadth, put his eye to the small end.

He remained for thirty or forty seconds, gazing attentively and silently. Then he drew himself up and said, in a husky voice:

"It's terrible. . . it's really terrible."

"What is?" she asked, anxiously.

"Look."

She bent down but the image was not clear to her and the telescope had to be focussed to suit her sight. The next moment she shuddered and said:

"It's two scarecrows, isn't it, both stuck up on the top? But why?"

"Look again," he said. "Look more carefully under the hats. . . the faces. . ."

"Oh!" she cried, turning faint with horror, "how awful!"

The field of the telescope, like the circular picture shown by a magic lantern, presented this spectacle: the platform of a broken tower, the walls of which were higher in the more distant part and formed as it were a back-drop, over which surged waves of ivy. In front, amid a cluster of bushes, were two human beings, a man and a woman, leaning back against a heap of fallen stones.

But the words man and woman could hardly be applied to these two forms, these two sinister puppets, which, it is true, wore clothes and hats—or rather shreds of clothes and remnants of hats—but had lost their eyes, their cheeks, their chins, every particle of flesh, until they were actually and positively nothing more than two skeletons.

"Two skeletons," stammered Hortense. "Two skeletons with clothes on. Who carried them up there?"

"Nobody."

"But still. . ."

"That man and that woman must have died at the top of the tower, years and years ago. . . and their flesh rotted under their clothes and the ravens ate them."

"But it's hideous, hideous!" cried Hortense, pale as death, her face drawn with horror.

HALF AN HOUR LATER, HORTENSE Daniel and Rénine left the Château de Halingre. Before their departure, they had gone as far as the ivy-grown tower, the remains of an old donjon-keep more than half demolished. The inside was empty. There seemed to have been a way of climbing to the top, at a comparatively recent period, by means of wooden stairs and ladders which now lay broken and scattered over the ground. The tower backed against the wall which marked the end of the park.

A curious fact, which surprised Hortense, was that Prince Rénine had neglected to pursue a more minute enquiry, as though the matter had lost all interest for him. He did not even speak of it any longer; and, in the inn at which they stopped and took a light meal in the nearest village, it was she who asked the landlord about the abandoned château. But she learnt nothing from him, for the man was new to the district and could give her no particulars. He did not even know the name of the owner.

They turned their horses' heads towards La Marèze. Again and again Hortense recalled the squalid sight which had met their eyes. But Rénine, who was in a lively mood and full of attentions to his companion, seemed utterly indifferent to those questions.

"But, after all," she exclaimed, impatiently, "we can't leave the matter there! It calls for a solution."

"As you say," he replied, "a solution is called for. M. Rossigny has to know where he stands and you have to decide what to do about him."

She shrugged her shoulders: "He's of no importance for the moment. The thing to-day. . ."

"Is what?"

"Is to know what those two dead bodies are."

"Still, Rossigny. . ."

"Rossigny can wait. But I can't. You have shown me a mystery which is now the only thing that matters. What do you intend to do?"

"To do?"

"Yes. There are two bodies. . . You'll inform the police, I suppose."

"Gracious goodness!" he exclaimed, laughing. "What for?"

"Well, there's a riddle that has to be cleared up at all costs, a terrible tragedy."

"We don't need any one to do that."

"What! Do you mean to say that you understand it?"

"Almost as plainly as though I had read it in a book, told in full detail, with explanatory illustrations. It's all so simple!"

She looked at him askance, wondering if he was making fun of her. But he seemed quite serious.

"Well?" she asked, quivering with curiosity.

MAURICE LEBLANC

The light was beginning to wane. They had trotted at a good pace; and the hunt was returning as they neared La Marèze.

"Well," he said, "we shall get the rest of our information from people living round about. . . from your uncle, for instance; and you will see how logically all the facts fit in. When you hold the first link of a chain, you are bound, whether you like it or not, to reach the last. It's the greatest fun in the world."

Once in the house, they separated. On going to her room, Hortense found her luggage and a furious letter from Rossigny in which he bade her good-bye and announced his departure.

Then Rénine knocked at her door:

"Your uncle is in the library," he said. "Will you go down with me? I've sent word that I am coming."

She went with him. He added:

"One word more. This morning, when I thwarted your plans and begged you to trust me, I naturally undertook an obligation towards you which I mean to fulfill without delay. I want to give you a positive proof of this."

She laughed:

"The only obligation which you took upon yourself was to satisfy my curiosity."

"It shall be satisfied," he assured her, gravely, "and more fully than you can possibly imagine."

M. d'Aigleroche was alone. He was smoking his pipe and drinking sherry. He offered a glass to Rénine, who refused.

"Well, Hortense!" he said, in a rather thick voice. "You know that it's pretty dull here, except in these September days. You must make the most of them. Have you had a pleasant ride with Rénine?"

"That's just what I wanted to talk about, my dear sir," interrupted the prince.

"You must excuse me, but I have to go to the station in ten minutes, to meet a friend of my wife's."

"Oh, ten minutes will be ample!"

"Just the time to smoke a cigarette?"

"No longer."

He took a cigarette from the case which M. d'Aigleroche handed to him, lit it and said:

"I must tell you that our ride happened to take us to an old domain which you are sure to know, the Domaine de Halingre."

"Certainly I know it. But it has been closed, boarded up for twenty-five years or so. You weren't able to get in, I suppose?"

"Yes, we were."

"Really? Was it interesting?"

"Extremely. We discovered the strangest things."

"What things?" asked the count, looking at his watch.

Rénine described what they had seen:

"On a tower some way from the house there were two dead bodies, two skeletons rather. . . a man and a woman still wearing the clothes which they had on when they were murdered."

"Come, come, now! Murdered?"

"Yes; and that is what we have come to trouble you about. The tragedy must date back to some twenty years ago. Was nothing known of it at the time?"

"Certainly not," declared the count. "I never heard of any such crime or disappearance."

"Oh, really!" said Rénine, looking a little disappointed. "I hoped to obtain a few particulars."

"I'm sorry."

"In that case, I apologise."

He consulted Hortense with a glance and moved towards the door. But on second thought:

"Could you not at least, my dear sir, bring me into touch with some persons in the neighbourhood, some members of your family, who might know more about it?"

"Of my family? And why?"

"Because the Domaine de Halingre used to belong and no doubt still belongs to the d'Aigleroches. The arms are an eagle on a heap of stones, on a rock. This at once suggested the connection."

This time the count appeared surprised. He pushed back his decanter and his glass of sherry and said:

"What's this you're telling me? I had no idea that we had any such neighbours."

Rénine shook his head and smiled:

"I should be more inclined to believe, sir, that you were not very eager to admit any relationship between yourself. . . and the unknown owner of the property."

"Then he's not a respectable man?"

"The man, to put it plainly, is a murderer."

"What do you mean?"

The count had risen from his chair. Hortense, greatly excited, said:

"Are you really sure that there has been a murder and that the murder was done by some one belonging to the house?"

"Quite sure."

"But why are you so certain?"

"Because I know who the two victims were and what caused them to be killed."

Prince Rénine was making none but positive statements and his method suggested the belief that he supported by the strongest proofs.

M. d'Aigleroche strode up and down the room, with his hands behind his back. He ended by saying:

"I always had an instinctive feeling that something had happened, but I never tried to find out. . . Now, as a matter of fact, twenty years ago, a relation of mine, a distant cousin, used to live at the Domaine de Halingre. I hoped, because of the name I bear, that this story, which, as I say, I never knew but suspected, would remain hidden for ever."

"So this cousin killed somebody?"

"Yes, he was obliged to."

Rénine shook his head:

"I am sorry to have to amend that phrase, my dear sir. The truth, on the contrary, is that your cousin took his victims' lives in cold blood and in a cowardly manner. I never heard of a crime more deliberately and craftily planned."

"What is it that you know?"

The moment had come for Rénine to explain himself, a solemn and anguish-stricken moment, the full gravity of which Hortense understood, though she had not yet divined any part of the tragedy which the prince unfolded step by step."

"It's a very simple story," he said. "There is every reason to believe that M. d'Aigleroche was married and that there was another couple living in the neighbourhood with whom the owner of the Domaine de Halingre were on friendly terms. What happened one day, which of these four persons first disturbed the relations between the two households, I am unable to say. But a likely version, which at once occurs to the mind, is that your cousin's wife, Madame d'Aigleroche, was in the habit of meeting the other husband in the ivy-covered tower, which had a door opening outside the estate. On discovering the intrigue, your cousin d'Aigleroche resolved to be revenged, but in such a manner that there should be no scandal and that no one even should ever know that the guilty pair had been killed. Now he had ascertained—as I did just now—that there was a part of the house, the belvedere, from which you can see, over the trees and the undulations of the park, the tower standing eight hundred yards away, and that this was the only place that overlooked the top of the tower. He therefore pierced a hole in the parapet, through one of the former loopholes, and from there, by using a telescope which fitted exactly in the grove which he had hollowed out, he watched the meetings of the two lovers. And it was from there, also, that, after carefully taking all his measurements, and calculating all his distances, on a Sunday, the 5th of September, when the house was empty, he killed them with two shots."

The truth was becoming apparent. The light of day was breaking. The count muttered:

"Yes, that's what must have happened. I expect that my cousin d'Aigleroche. . ."

"The murderer," Rénine continued, "stopped up the loophole neatly with a clod of earth. No one would ever know that two dead bodies were decaying on the top of that tower which was never visited and of which he took the precaution to demolish the wooden stairs. Nothing therefore remained for him to do but to explain the disappearance of his wife and his friend. This presented no difficulty. He accused them of having eloped together."

Hortense gave a start. Suddenly, as though the last sentence were a complete and to her an absolutely unexpected revelation, she understood what Rénine was trying to convey:

"What do you mean?" she asked.

"I mean that M. d'Aigleroche accused his wife and his friend of eloping together."

"No, no!" she cried. "I can't allow that! . . . You are speaking of a cousin of my uncle's? Why mix up the two stories?"

"Why mix up this story with another which took place at that time?" said the prince. "But I am not mixing them up, my dear madame; there is only one story and I am telling it as it happened."

Hortense turned to her uncle. He sat silent, with his arms folded; and his head remained in the shadow cast by the lamp-shade. Why had he not protested?

Rénine repeated in a firm tone:

"There is only one story. On the evening of that very day, the 5th of September at eight o'clock, M. d'Aigleroche, doubtless alleging as his reason that he was going in pursuit of the runaway couple, left his house after boarding up the entrance. He went away, leaving all the rooms as they were and removing only the firearms from their glass case. At the last minute, he had a presentiment, which has been justified to-day, that the discovery of the telescope which had played so great a part in the preparation of his crime might serve as a clue to an enquiry; and he threw it into the clock-case, where, as luck would have it, it interrupted the swing of the pendulum. This unreflecting action, one of those which every criminal inevitably commits, was to betray him twenty years later. Just now, the blows which I struck to force the door of the drawing-room released the pendulum. The clock was set going, struck eight o'clock. . . and I possessed the clue of thread which was to lead me through the labyrinth."

"Proofs!" stammered Hortense. "Proofs!"

"Proofs?" replied Rénine, in a loud voice. "Why, there are any number of proofs; and you know them as well as I do. Who could have killed at that distance of eight hundred yards, except an expert shot, an ardent sportsman? You agree, M. d'Aigleroche, do you not? . . . Proofs? Why was nothing removed from the house, nothing except the guns, those guns which an ardent sportsman cannot afford to leave behind—you agree, M. d'Aigleroche—those guns which we find here, hanging in trophies on the walls! . . . Proofs? What about that date, the 5th of September, which was the date of the crime and which has left such a horrible memory in the criminal's mind that every year at this time—at this time alone—he surrounds himself with distractions and that every year, on this same 5th of September, he forgets his habits of temperance? Well, to-day, is the 5th of September. . . Proofs? Why, if there weren't any others, would that not be enough for you?"

And Rénine, flinging out his arm, pointed to the Comte d'Aigleroche, who, terrified by this evocation of the past, had sunk huddled into a chair and was hiding his head in his hands.

Hortense did not attempt to argue with him. She had never liked her uncle, or rather her husband's uncle. She now accepted the accusation laid against him.

Sixty seconds passed. Then M. d'Aigleroche walked up to them and said:

"Whether the story be true or not, you can't call a husband a criminal for avenging his honour and killing his faithless wife."

"No," replied Rénine, "but I have told only the first version of the story. There is another which is infinitely more serious. . . and more probable, one to which a more thorough investigation would be sure to lead."

"What do you mean?"

"I mean this. It may not be a matter of a husband taking the law into his own hands, as I charitably supposed. It may be a matter of a ruined man who covets his friend's money and his friend's wife and who, with this object in view, to secure his freedom, to get rid of his friend and of his own wife, draws them into a trap, suggests to them that they should visit that lonely tower and kills them by shooting them from a distance safely under cover."

"No, no," the count protested. "No, all that is untrue."

"I don't say it isn't. I am basing my accusation on proofs, but also on intuitions and arguments which up to now have been extremely accurate. All the same, I admit that the second version may be incorrect. But, if so, why feel any remorse? One does not feel remorse for punishing guilty people."

"One does for taking life. It is a crushing burden to bear."

"Was it to give himself greater strength to bear this burden that M. d'Aigleroche afterwards married his victim's widow? For that, sir, is the crux of the question. What was the motive of that marriage? Was M. d'Aigleroche penniless? Was the woman he was taking as his second wife rich? Or were they both in love with each other and did M. d'Aigleroche plan with her to kill his first wife and the husband of his second wife? These are problems to which I do not know the answer. They have no interest for the moment; but the police, with all the means at their disposal, would have no great difficulty in elucidating them."

M. d'Aigleroche staggered and had to steady himself against the back of a chair. Livid in the face, he spluttered:

"Are you going to inform the police?"

"No, no," said Rénine. "To begin with, there is the statute of limitations. Then there are twenty years of remorse and dread, a memory which will pursue the criminal to his dying hour, accompanied no doubt by domestic discord, hatred, a daily hell. . . and, in the end, the necessity of returning to the tower and removing the traces of the two murders, the frightful punishment of climbing that tower, of touching those skeletons, of undressing them and burying them. That will be enough. We will not ask for more. We will not give it to the public to batten on and create a scandal which would recoil upon M. d'Aigleroche's niece. No, let us leave this disgraceful business alone."

The count resumed his seat at the table, with his hands clutching his forehead, and asked:

"Then why. . . ?"

"Why do I interfere?" said Rénine. "What you mean is that I must have had some object in speaking. That is so. There must indeed be a penalty, however slight, and our interview must lead to some practical result. But have no fear: M. d'Aigleroche will be let off lightly."

The contest was ended. The count felt that he had only a small formality to fulfil, a sacrifice to accept; and, recovering some of his self-assurance, he said, in an almost sarcastic tone:

"What's your price?"

Rénine burst out laughing:

"Splendid! You see the position. Only, you make a mistake in drawing me into the business. I'm working for the glory of the thing."

"In that case?"

"You will be called upon at most to make restitution."

"Restitution?"

Rénine leant over the table and said:

"In one of those drawers is a deed awaiting your signature. It is a draft agreement between you and your niece Hortense Daniel, relating to her private fortune, which fortune was squandered and for which you are responsible. Sign the deed."

M. d'Aigleroche gave a start:

"Do you know the amount?"

"I don't wish to know it."

"And if I refuse? . . ."

"I shall ask to see the Comtesse d'Aigleroche."

Without further hesitation, the count opened a drawer, produced a document on stamped paper and quickly signed it:

"Here you are," he said, "and I hope. . ."

"You hope, as I do, that you and I may never have any future dealings? I'm convinced of it. I shall leave this evening; your niece, no doubt, tomorrow. Good-bye."

IN THE DRAWING-ROOM, WHICH WAS still empty, while the guests at the house were dressing for dinner, Rénine handed the deed to Hortense. She seemed dazed by all that she had heard; and the thing that bewildered her even more than the relentless light shed upon her uncle's past was the miraculous insight and amazing lucidity displayed by this man: the man who for some hours had controlled events and conjured up before her eyes the actual scenes of a tragedy which no one had beheld.

"Are you satisfied with me?" he asked.

She gave him both her hands:

"You have saved me from Rossigny. You have given me back my freedom and my independence. I thank you from the bottom of my heart."

"Oh, that's not what I am asking you to say!" he answered. "My first and main object was to amuse you. Your life seemed so humdrum and lacking in the unexpected. Has it been so to-day?"

"How can you ask such a question? I have had the strangest and most stirring experiences."

"That is life," he said. "When one knows how to use one's eyes. Adventure exists everywhere, in the meanest hovel, under the mask of the wisest of men. Everywhere, if you are only willing, you will find an excuse for excitement, for doing good, for saving a victim, for ending an injustice."

Impressed by his power and authority, she murmured:

"Who are you exactly?"

"An adventurer. Nothing more. A lover of adventures. Life is not worth living except in moments of adventure, the adventures of others or personal adventures. To-day's has upset you because it affected the innermost depths of your being. But those of others are no less stimulating. Would you like to make the experiment?"

"How?"

"Become the companion of my adventures. If any one calls on me for help, help him with me. If chance or instinct puts me on the track of a crime or the trace of a sorrow, let us both set out together. Do you consent?"

"Yes," she said, "but. . ."

She hesitated, as though trying to guess Rénine's secret intentions.

"But," he said, expressing her thoughts for her, with a smile, "you are a trifle sceptical. What you are saying to yourself is, 'How far does that lover of adventures want to make me go? It is quite obvious that I attract him; and sooner or later he would not be sorry to receive payment for his services.' You are quite right. We must have a formal contract."

"Very formal," said Hortense, preferring to give a jesting tone to the conversation. "Let me hear your proposals."

　　　　　　　　　　　MAURICE LEBLANC

He reflected for a moment and continued:

"Well, we'll say this. The clock at Halingre gave eight strokes this afternoon, the day of the first adventure. Will you accept its decree and agree to carry out seven more of these delightful enterprises with me, during a period, for instance, of three months? And shall we say that, at the eighth, you will be pledged to grant me. . ."

"What?"

He deferred his answer:

"Observe that you will always be at liberty to leave me on the road if I do not succeed in interesting you. But, if you accompany me to the end, if you allow me to begin and complete the eighth enterprise with you, in three months, on the 5th of December, at the very moment when the eighth stroke of that clock sounds—and it will sound, you may be sure of that, for the old brass pendulum will not stop swinging again—you will be pledged to grant me. . ."

"What?" she repeated, a little unnerved by waiting.

He was silent. He looked at the beautiful lips which he had meant to claim as his reward. He felt perfectly certain that Hortense had understood and he thought it unnecessary to speak more plainly:

"The mere delight of seeing you will be enough to satisfy me. It is not for me but for you to impose conditions. Name them: what do you demand?"

She was grateful for his respect and said, laughingly:

"What do I demand?"

"Yes."

"Can I demand anything I like, however difficult and impossible?"

"Everything is easy and everything is possible to the man who is bent on winning you."

Then she said:

"I demand that you shall restore to me a small, antique clasp, made of a cornelian set in a silver mount. It came to me from my mother and everyone knew that it used to bring her happiness and me too. Since the day when it vanished from my jewel-case, I have had nothing but unhappiness. Restore it to me, my good genius."

"When was the clasp stolen?"

She answered gaily:

"Seven years ago. . . or eight. . . or nine; I don't know exactly. . . I don't know where. . . I don't know how. . . I know nothing about it. . ."

"I will find it," Rénine declared, "and you shall be happy."

II

The Water-Bottle

Four days after she had settled down in Paris, Hortense Daniel agreed to meet Prince Rénine in the Bois. It was a glorious morning and they sat down on the terrace of the Restaurant Impérial, a little to one side.

Hortense, feeling glad to be alive, was in a playful mood, full of attractive grace. Rénine, lest he should startle her, refrained from alluding to the compact into which they had entered at his suggestion. She told him how she had left La Marèze and said that she had not heard of Rossigny.

"I have," said Rénine. "I've heard of him."

"Oh?"

"Yes, he sent me a challenge. We fought a duel this morning. Rossigny got a scratch in the shoulder. That finished the duel. Let's talk of something else."

There was no further mention of Rossigny. Rénine at once expounded to Hortense the plan of two enterprises which he had in view and in which he offered, with no great enthusiasm, to let her share:

"The finest adventure," he declared, "is that which we do not foresee. It comes unexpectedly, unannounced; and no one, save the initiated, realizes that an opportunity to act and to expend one's energies is close at hand. It has to be seized at once. A moment's hesitation may mean that we are too late. We are warned by a special sense, like that of a sleuth-hound which distinguishes the right scent from all the others that cross it."

The terrace was beginning to fill up around them. At the next table sat a young man reading a newspaper. They were able to see his insignificant profile and his long, dark moustache. From behind them, through an open window of the restaurant, came the distant strains of a band; in one of the rooms a few couples were dancing.

As Rénine was paying for the refreshments, the young man with the long moustache stifled a cry and, in a choking voice, called one of the waiters:

"What do I owe you? . . . No change? Oh, good Lord, hurry up!"

Rénine, without a moment's hesitation, had picked up the paper. After casting a swift glance down the page, he read, under his breath:

"Maître Dourdens, the counsel for the defence in the trial of Jacques Aubrieux, has been received at the Élysée. We are informed that the President of the Republic has refused to reprieve the condemned man and that the execution will take place to-morrow morning."

After crossing the terrace, the young man found himself faced, at the entrance to the garden, by a lady and gentleman who blocked his way; and the latter said:

"Excuse me, sir, but I noticed your agitation. It's about Jacques Aubrieux, isn't it?"

"Yes, yes, Jacques Aubrieux," the young man stammered. "Jacques, the friend of my childhood. I'm hurrying to see his wife. She must be beside herself with grief."

"Can I offer you my assistance? I am Prince Rénine. This lady and I would be happy to call on Madame Aubrieux and to place our services at her disposal."

The young man, upset by the news which he had read, seemed not to understand. He introduced himself awkwardly:

"My name is Dutreuil, Gaston Dutreuil."

Rénine beckoned to his chauffeur, who was waiting at some little distance, and pushed Gaston Dutreuil into the car, asking:

"What address? Where does Madame Aubrieux live?"

"23 *bis*, Avenue du Roule."

After helping Hortense in, Rénine repeated the address to the chauffeur and, as soon as they drove off, tried to question Gaston Dutreuil:

"I know very little of the case," he said. "Tell it to me as briefly as you can. Jacques Aubrieux killed one of his near relations, didn't he?"

"He is innocent, sir," replied the young man, who seemed incapable of giving the least explanation. "Innocent, I swear it. I've been Jacques' friend for twenty years. . . He is innocent. . . and it would be monstrous. . ."

There was nothing to be got out of him. Besides, it was only a short drive. They entered Neuilly through the Porte des Sablons and, two minutes later, stopped before a long, narrow passage between high walls which led them to a small, one-storeyed house.

Gaston Dutreuil rang.

"Madame is in the drawing-room, with her mother," said the maid who opened the door.

"I'll go in to the ladies," he said, taking Rénine and Hortense with him.

It was a fair-sized, prettily-furnished room, which, in ordinary times, must have been used also as a study. Two women sat weeping, one of whom, elderly and grey-haired, came up to Gaston Dutreuil. He explained the reason for Rénine's presence and she at once cried, amid her sobs:

"My daughter's husband is innocent, sir. Jacques? A better man never lived. He was so good-hearted! Murder his cousin? But he worshipped his cousin! I swear that he's not guilty, sir! And they are going to commit the infamy of putting him to death? Oh, sir, it will kill my daughter!"

Rénine realized that all these people had been living for months under the obsession of that innocence and in the certainty that an innocent man could never be executed. The news of the execution, which was now inevitable, was driving them mad.

He went up to a poor creature bent in two whose face, a quite young face, framed in pretty, flaxen hair, was convulsed with desperate grief. Hortense, who had already taken a seat beside her, gently drew her head against her shoulder. Rénine said to her:

"Madame, I do not know what I can do for you. But I give you my word of honour that, if any one in this world can be of use to you, it is myself. I therefore implore you to answer my questions as though the clear and definite wording of your replies were able to alter the aspect of things and as though you wished to make me share your opinion of Jacques Aubrieux. For he is innocent, is he not?"

"Oh, sir, indeed he is!" she exclaimed; and the woman's whole soul was in the words.

"You are certain of it. But you were unable to communicate your certainty to the court. Well, you must now compel me to share it. I am not asking you to go into details and to live again through the hideous torment which you have suffered, but merely to answer certain questions. Will you do this?"

"I will."

Rénine's influence over her was complete. With a few sentences Rénine had succeeded in subduing her and inspiring her with the will to obey. And once more Hortense realized all the man's power, authority and persuasion.

"What was your husband?" he asked, after begging the mother and Gaston Dutreuil to preserve absolute silence.

"An insurance-broker."

"Lucky in business?"

"Until last year, yes."

"So there have been financial difficulties during the past few months?"

"Yes."

"And the murder was committed when?"

"Last March, on a Sunday."

"Who was the victim?"

"A distant cousin, M. Guillaume, who lived at Suresnes."

"What was the sum stolen?"

"Sixty thousand-franc notes, which this cousin had received the day before, in payment of a long-outstanding debt."

"Did your husband know that?"

"Yes. His cousin told him of it on the Sunday, in the course of a conversation on the telephone, and Jacques insisted that his cousin ought not to keep so large a sum in the house and that he ought to pay it into a bank next day."

"Was this in the morning?"

"At one o'clock in the afternoon. Jacques was to have gone to M. Guillaume on his motor-cycle. But he felt tired and told him that he would not go out. So he remained here all day."

"Alone?"

"Yes. The two servants were out. I went to the Cinéma des Ternes with my mother and our friend Dutreuil. In the evening, we learnt that M. Guillaume had been murdered. Next morning, Jacques was arrested."

"On what evidence?"

The poor creature hesitated to reply: the evidence of guilt had evidently been overwhelming. Then, obeying a sign from Rénine, she answered without a pause:

"The murderer went to Suresnes on a motorcycle and the tracks discovered were those of my husband's machine. They found a handkerchief with my husband's initials; and the revolver which was used belonged to him. Lastly, one of our neighbours maintains that he saw my husband go out on his bicycle at three o'clock and another that he saw him come in at half-past four. The murder was committed at four o'clock."

"And what does Jacques Aubrieux say in his defence?"

"He declares that he slept all the afternoon. During that time, some one came who managed to unlock the cycle-shed and take the motor-cycle to go to Suresnes. As for the handkerchief and the revolver, they were in the tool-bag. There would be nothing surprising in the murderer's using them."

"It seems a plausible explanation."

"Yes, but the prosecution raised two objections. In the first place, nobody, absolutely nobody, knew that my husband was going to stay at home all day, because, on the contrary, it was his habit to go out on his motor-cycle every Sunday afternoon."

"And the second objection?"

She flushed and murmured:

"The murderer went to the pantry at M. Guillaume's and drank half a bottle of wine straight out of the bottle, which shows my husband's fingerprints."

It seemed as though her strength was exhausted and as though, at the same time, the unconscious hope which Rénine's intervention had awakened in her had suddenly vanished before the accumulation of adverse facts. Again she collapsed, withdrawn into a sort of silent meditation from which Hortense's affectionate attentions were unable to distract her.

The mother stammered:

"He's not guilty, is he, sir? And they can't punish an innocent man. They haven't the right to kill my daughter. Oh dear, oh dear, what have we done to be tortured like this? My poor little Madeleine!"

"She will kill herself," said Dutreuil, in a scared voice. "She will never be able to endure the idea that they are guillotining Jacques. She will kill herself presently. . . this very night. . ."

Rénine was striding up and down the room.

"You can do nothing for her, can you?" asked Hortense.

"It's half-past eleven now," he replied, in an anxious tone, "and it's to happen to-morrow morning."

"Do you think he's guilty?"

"I don't know. . . I don't know. . . The poor woman's conviction is too impressive to be neglected. When two people have lived together for years, they can hardly be mistaken about each other to that degree. And yet. . ."

He stretched himself out on a sofa and lit a cigarette. He smoked three in succession, without a word from any one to interrupt his train

MAURICE LEBLANC

of thought. From time to time he looked at his watch. Every minute was of such importance!

At last he went back to Madeleine Aubrieux, took her hands and said, very gently:

"You must not kill yourself. There is hope left until the last minute has come; and I promise you that, for my part, I will not be disheartened until that last minute. But I need your calmness and your confidence."

"I will be calm," she said, with a pitiable air.

"And confident?"

"And confident."

"Well, wait for me. I shall be back in two hours from now. Will you come with us, M. Dutreuil?"

As they were stepping into his car, he asked the young man:

"Do you know any small, unfrequented restaurant, not too far inside Paris?"

"There's the Brasserie Lutetia, on the ground-floor of the house in which I live, on the Place des Ternes."

"Capital. That will be very handy."

They scarcely spoke on the way. Rénine, however, said to Gaston Dutreuil:

"So far as I remember, the numbers of the notes are known, aren't they?"

"Yes. M. Guillaume had entered the sixty numbers in his pocket-book."

Rénine muttered, a moment later:

"That's where the whole problem lies. Where are the notes? If we could lay our hands on them, we should know everything."

At the Brasserie Lutetia there was a telephone in the private room where he asked to have lunch served. When the waiter had left him alone with Hortense and Dutreuil, he took down the receiver with a resolute air:

"Hullo! . . . Prefecture of police, please. . . Hullo! Hullo! . . . Is that the Prefecture of police? Please put me on to the criminal investigation department. I have a very important communication to make. You can say it's Prince Rénine."

Holding the receiver in his hand, he turned to Gaston Dutreuil:

"I can ask some one to come here, I suppose? We shall be quite undisturbed?"

"Quite."

He listened again:

"The secretary to the head of the criminal investigation department? Oh, excellent! Mr. Secretary, I have on several occasions been in communication with M. Dudouis and have given him information which has been of great use to him. He is sure to remember Prince Rénine. I may be able to-day to show him where the sixty thousand-franc notes are hidden which Aubrieux the murderer stole from his cousin. If he's interested in the proposal, beg him to send an inspector to the Brasserie Lutetia, Place des Ternes. I shall be there with a lady and M. Dutreuil, Aubrieux's friend. Good day, Mr. Secretary."

When Rénine hung up the instrument, he saw the amazed faces of Hortense and of Gaston Dutreuil confronting him.

Hortense whispered:

"Then you know? You've discovered. . . ?"

"Nothing," he said, laughing.

"Well?"

"Well, I'm acting as though I knew. It's not a bad method. Let's have some lunch, shall we?"

The clock marked a quarter to one.

"The man from the prefecture will be here," he said, "in twenty minutes at latest."

"And if no one comes?" Hortense objected.

"That would surprise me. Of course, if I had sent a message to M. Dudouis saying, 'Aubrieux is innocent,' I should have failed to make any impression. It's not the least use, on the eve of an execution, to attempt to convince the gentry of the police or of the law that a man condemned to death is innocent. No. From henceforth Jacques Aubrieux belongs to the executioner. But the prospect of securing the sixty bank-notes is a windfall worth taking a little trouble over. Just think: that was the weak point in the indictment, those sixty notes which they were unable to trace."

"But, as you know nothing of their whereabouts. . ."

"My dear girl—I hope you don't mind my calling you so?—my dear girl, when a man can't explain this or that physical phenomenon, he adopts some sort of theory which explains the various manifestations of the phenomenon and says that everything happened as though the theory were correct. That's what I am doing."

"That amounts to saying that you are going upon a supposition?"

Rénine did not reply. Not until some time later, when lunch was over, did he say:

"Obviously I am going upon a supposition. If I had several days before me, I should take the trouble of first verifying my theory, which is based upon intuition quite as much as upon a few scattered facts. But I have only two hours; and I am embarking on the unknown path as though I were certain that it would lead me to the truth."

"And suppose you are wrong?"

"I have no choice. Besides, it is too late. There's a knock. Oh, one word more! Whatever I may say, don't contradict me. Nor you, M. Dutreuil."

He opened the door. A thin man, with a red imperial, entered:

"Prince Rénine?"

"Yes, sir. You, of course, are from M. Dudouis?"

"Yes."

And the newcomer gave his name:

"Chief-inspector Morisseau."

"I am obliged to you for coming so promptly, Mr. Chief-inspector," said Prince Rénine, "and I hope that M. Dudouis will not regret having placed you at my disposal."

"At your entire disposal, in addition to two inspectors whom I have left in the square outside and who have been in the case, with me, from the first."

"I shall not detain you for any length of time," said Rénine, "and I will not even ask you to sit down. We have only a few minutes in which to settle everything. You know what it's all about?"

"The sixty thousand-franc notes stolen from M. Guillaume. I have the numbers here."

Rénine ran his eyes down the slip of paper which the chief-inspector handed him and said:

"That's right. The two lists agree."

Inspector Morisseau seemed greatly excited:

"The chief attaches the greatest importance to your discovery. So you will be able to show me? . . ."

Rénine was silent for a moment and then declared:

"Mr. Chief-inspector, a personal investigation—and a most exhaustive investigation it was, as I will explain to you presently—has revealed the fact that, on his return from Suresnes, the murderer, after replacing the motor-cycle in the shed in the Avenue du Roule, ran to the Ternes and entered this house."

"This house?"

"Yes."

"But what did he come here for?"

"To hide the proceeds of his theft, the sixty bank-notes."

"How do you mean? Where?"

"In a flat of which he had the key, on the fifth floor."

Gaston Dutreuil exclaimed, in amazement:

"But there's only one flat on the fifth floor and that's the one I live in!"

"Exactly; and, as you were at the cinema with Madame Aubrieux and her mother, advantage was taken of your absence. . ."

"Impossible! No one has the key except myself."

"One can get in without a key."

"But I have seen no marks of any kind."

Morisseau intervened:

"Come, let us understand one another. You say the bank-notes were hidden in M. Dutreuil's flat?"

"Yes."

"Then, as Jacques Aubrieux was arrested the next morning, the notes ought to be there still?"

"That's my opinion."

Gaston Dutreuil could not help laughing:

"But that's absurd! I should have found them!"

"Did you look for them?"

"No. But I should have come across them at any moment. The place isn't big enough to swing a cat in. Would you care to see it?"

"However small it may be, it's large enough to hold sixty bits of paper."

"Of course, everything is possible," said Dutreuil. "Still, I must repeat that nobody, to my knowledge, has been to my rooms; that there is only one key; that I am my own housekeeper; and that I can't quite understand. . ."

Hortense too could not understand. With her eyes fixed on Prince Rénine's, she was trying to read his innermost thoughts. What game was he playing? Was it her duty to support his statements? She ended by saying:

"Mr. Chief-inspector, since Prince Rénine maintains that the notes have been put away upstairs, wouldn't the simplest thing be to go and look? M. Dutreuil will take us up, won't you?"

"This minute," said the young man. "As you say, that will be simplest."

They all four climbed the five storys of the house and, after Dutreuil had opened the door, entered a tiny set of chambers consisting of a sitting-room, bedroom, kitchen and bathroom, all arranged with fastidious neatness. It was easy to see that every chair in the sitting-room occupied a definite place. The pipes had a rack to themselves; so had the matches. Three walking-sticks, arranged according to their length, hung from three nails. On a little table before the window a hat-box, filled with tissue-paper, awaited the felt hat which Dutreuil carefully placed in it. He laid his gloves beside it, on the lid.

He did all this with sedate and mechanical movements, like a man who loves to see things in the places which he has chosen for them. Indeed, no sooner did Rénine shift something than Dutreuil made a slight gesture of protest, took out his hat again, stuck it on his head, opened the window and rested his elbows on the sill, with his back turned to the room, as though he were unable to bear the sight of such vandalism.

"You're positive, are you not?" the inspector asked Rénine.

"Yes, yes, I'm positive that the sixty notes were brought here after the murder."

"Let's look for them."

This was easy and soon done. In half an hour, not a corner remained unexplored, not a knick-knack unlifted.

"Nothing," said Inspector Morisseau. "Shall we continue?"

"No," replied Rénine, "The notes are no longer here."

"What do you mean?"

"I mean that they have been removed."

"By whom? Can't you make a more definite accusation?"

Rénine did not reply. But Gaston Dutreuil wheeled round. He was choking and spluttered:

"Mr. Inspector, would you like *me* to make the accusation more definite, as conveyed by this gentleman's remarks? It all means that there's a dishonest man here, that the notes hidden by the murderer were discovered and stolen by that dishonest man and deposited in another and safer place. That is your idea, sir, is it not? And you accuse me of committing this theft don't you?"

He came forward, drumming his chest with his fists: "Me! Me! I found the notes, did I, and kept them for myself? You dare to suggest that!"

Rénine still made no reply. Dutreuil flew into a rage and, taking Inspector Morisseau aside, exclaimed:

"Mr. Inspector, I strongly protest against all this farce and against the part which you are unconsciously playing in it. Before your arrival, Prince Rénine told this lady and myself that he knew nothing, that he was venturing into this affair at random and that he was following the first road that offered, trusting to luck. Do you deny it, sir?"

Rénine did not open his lips.

"Answer me, will you? Explain yourself; for, really, you are putting forward the most improbable facts without any proof whatever. It's easy enough to say that I stole the notes. And how were you to know that they were here at all? Who brought them here? Why should the murderer choose this flat to hide them in? It's all so stupid, so illogical and absurd! . . . Give us your proofs, sir. . . one single proof!"

Inspector Morisseau seemed perplexed. He questioned Rénine with a glance. Rénine said:

"Since you want specific details, we will get them from Madame Aubrieux herself. She's on the telephone. Let's go downstairs. We shall know all about it in a minute."

Dutreuil shrugged his shoulders:

"As you please; but what a waste of time!"

He seemed greatly irritated. His long wait at the window, under a blazing sun, had thrown him into a sweat. He went to his bedroom and returned with a bottle of water, of which he took a few sips, afterwards placing the bottle on the window-sill:

"Come along," he said.

Prince Rénine chuckled.

"You seem to be in a hurry to leave the place."

"I'm in a hurry to show you up," retorted Dutreuil, slamming the door.

They went downstairs to the private room containing the telephone. The room was empty. Rénine asked Gaston Dutreuil for the Aubrieuxs' number, took down the instrument and was put through.

The maid who came to the telephone answered that Madame Aubrieux had fainted, after giving way to an access of despair, and that she was now asleep.

"Fetch her mother, please. Prince Rénine speaking. It's urgent."

He handed the second receiver to Morisseau. For that matter, the voices were so distinct that Dutreuil and Hortense were able to hear every word exchanged.

"Is that you, madame?"

"Yes. Prince Rénine, I believe?"

"Prince Rénine."

"Oh, sir, what news have you for me? Is there any hope?" asked the old lady, in a tone of entreaty.

"The enquiry is proceeding very satisfactorily," said Rénine, "and you may hope for the best. For the moment, I want you to give me some very important particulars. On the day of the murder, did Gaston Dutreuil come to your house?"

"Yes, he came to fetch my daughter and myself, after lunch."

"Did he know at the time that M. Guillaume had sixty thousand francs at his place?"

"Yes, I told him."

"And that Jacques Aubrieux was not feeling very well and was proposing not to take his usual cycle-ride but to stay at home and sleep?"

"Yes."

"You are sure?"

"Absolutely certain."

"And you all three went to the cinema together?"

"Yes."

"And you were all sitting together?"

"Oh, no! There was no room. He took a seat farther away."

"A seat where you could see him?"

"No."

"But he came to you during the interval?"

"No, we did not see him until we were going out."

"There is no doubt of that?"

"None at all."

"Very well, madame. I will tell you the result of my efforts in an hour's time. But above all, don't wake up Madame Aubrieux."

"And suppose she wakes of her own accord?"

"Reassure her and give her confidence. Everything is going well, very well indeed."

He hung up the receiver and turned to Dutreuil, laughing:

"Ha, ha, my boy! Things are beginning to look clearer. What do you say?"

It was difficult to tell what these words meant or what conclusions Rénine had drawn from his conversation. The silence was painful and oppressive.

"Mr. Chief-Inspector, you have some of your men outside, haven't you?"

"Two detective-sergeants."

"It's important that they should be there. Please also ask the manager not to disturb us on any account."

And, when Morisseau returned, Rénine closed the door, took his stand in front of Dutreuil and, speaking in a good-humoured but emphatic tone, said:

"It amounts to this, young man, that the ladies saw nothing of you between three and five o'clock on that Sunday. That's rather a curious detail."

"A perfectly natural detail," Dutreuil retorted, "and one, moreover, which proves nothing at all."

"It proves, young man, that you had a good two hours at your disposal."

"Obviously. Two hours which I spent at the cinema."

"Or somewhere else."

Dutreuil looked at him:

"Somewhere else?"

"Yes. As you were free, you had plenty of time to go wherever you liked. . . to Suresnes, for instance."

"Oh!" said the young man, jesting in his turn. "Suresnes is a long way off!"

"It's quite close! Hadn't you your friend Jacques Aubrieux's motor-cycle?"

A fresh pause followed these words. Dutreuil had knitted his brows as though he were trying to understand. At last he was heard to whisper:

"So that is what he was trying to lead up to! . . . The brute! . . ."

Rénine brought down his hand on Dutreuil's shoulder:

"No more talk! Facts! Gaston Dutreuil, you are the only person who on that day knew two essential things: first, that Cousin Guillaume had sixty thousand francs in his house; secondly, that Jacques Aubrieux was not going out. You at once saw your chance. The motor-cycle was available. You slipped out during the performance. You went to Suresnes. You killed Cousin Guillaume. You took the sixty bank-notes and left them at your rooms. And at five o'clock you went back to fetch the ladies."

Dutreuil had listened with an expression at once mocking and flurried, casting an occasional glance at Inspector Morisseau as though to enlist him as a witness:

"The man's mad," it seemed to say. "It's no use being angry with him."

When Rénine had finished, he began to laugh:

"Very funny! . . . A capital joke! . . . So it was I whom the neighbours saw going and returning on the motor-cycle?"

"It was you disguised in Jacques Aubrieux's clothes."

"And it was my finger-prints that were found on the bottle in M. Guillaume's pantry?"

"The bottle had been opened by Jacques Aubrieux at lunch, in his own house, and it was you who took it with you to serve as evidence."

"Funnier and funnier!" cried Dutreuil, who had the air of being frankly amused. "Then I contrived the whole affair so that Jacques Aubrieux might be accused of the crime?"

"It was the safest means of not being accused yourself."

"Yes, but Jacques is a friend whom I have known from childhood."

"You're in love with his wife."

The young man gave a sudden, infuriated start:

"You dare! . . . What! You dare make such an infamous suggestion?"

"I have proof of it."

"That's a lie! I have always respected Madeleine Aubrieux and revered her. . ."

"Apparently. But you're in love with her. You desire her. Don't contradict me. I have abundant proof of it."

"That's a lie, I tell you! You have only known me a few hours!"

"Come, come! I've been quietly watching you for days, waiting for the moment to pounce upon you."

He took the young man by the shoulders and shook him:

"Come, Dutreuil, confess! I hold all the proofs in my hand. I have witnesses whom we shall meet presently at the criminal investigation department. Confess, can't you? In spite of everything, you're tortured by remorse. Remember your dismay, at the restaurant, when you had seen the newspaper. What? Jacques Aubrieux condemned to die? That's more than you bargained for! Penal servitude would have suited your book; but the scaffold! . . . Jacques Aubrieux executed to-morrow, an innocent man! . . . Confess, won't you? Confess to save your own skin! Own up!"

Bending over the other, he was trying with all his might to extort a confession from him. But Dutreuil drew himself up and coldly, with a sort of scorn in his voice, said:

"Sir, you are a madman. Not a word that you have said has any sense in it. All your accusations are false. What about the bank-notes? Did you find them at my place as you said you would?"

Rénine, exasperated, clenched his fist in his face:

"Oh, you swine, I'll dish you yet, I swear I will!"

He drew the inspector aside:

"Well, what do you say to it? An arrant rogue, isn't he?"

The inspector nodded his head:

"It may be. . . But, all the same. . . so far there's no real evidence."

"Wait, M. Morisseau," said Rénine. "Wait until we've had our interview with M. Dudouis. For we shall see M. Dudouis at the prefecture, shall we not?"

"Yes, he'll be there at three o'clock."

"Well, you'll be convinced, Mr. Inspector! I tell you here and now that you will be convinced."

Rénine was chuckling like a man who feels certain of the course of events. Hortense, who was standing near him and was able to speak to him without being heard by the others, asked, in a low voice:

"You've got him, haven't you?"

He nodded his head in assent:

"Got him? I should think I have! All the same, I'm no farther forward than I was at the beginning."

"But this is awful! And your proofs?"

"Not the shadow of a proof. . . I was hoping to trip him up. But he's kept his feet, the rascal!"

"Still, you're certain it's he?"

"It can't be any one else. I had an intuition at the very outset; and I've not taken my eyes off him since. I have seen his anxiety increasing as my investigations seemed to centre on him and concern him more closely. Now I know."

"And he's in love with Madame Aubrieux?"

"In logic, he's bound to be. But so far we have only hypothetical suppositions, or rather certainties which are personal to myself. We shall never intercept the guillotine with those. Ah, if we could only find the bank-notes! Given the bank-notes, M. Dudouis would act. Without them, he will laugh in my face."

"What then?" murmured Hortense, in anguished accents.

He did not reply. He walked up and down the room, assuming an air of gaiety and rubbing his hands. All was going so well! It was really a treat to take up a case which, so to speak, worked itself out automatically.

"Suppose we went on to the prefecture, M. Morisseau? The chief must be there by now. And, having gone so far, we may as well finish. Will M. Dutreuil come with us?"

"Why not?" said Dutreuil, arrogantly.

But, just as Rénine was opening the door, there was a noise in the passage and the manager ran up, waving his arms:

"Is M. Dutreuil still here? . . . M. Dutreuil, your flat is on fire! . . . A man outside told us. He saw it from the square."

The young man's eyes lit up. For perhaps half a second his mouth was twisted by a smile which Rénine noticed:

"Oh, you ruffian!" he cried. "You've given yourself away, my beauty! It was you who set fire to the place upstairs; and now the notes are burning."

He blocked his exit.

"Let me pass," shouted Dutreuil. "There's a fire and no one can get in, because no one else has a key. Here it is. Let me pass, damn it!"

Rénine snatched the key from his hand and, holding him by the collar of his coat:

"Don't you move, my fine fellow! The game's up! You precious blackguard! M. Morisseau, will you give orders to the sergeant not to let him out of his sight and to blow out his brains if he tries to get away? Sergeant, we rely on you! Put a bullet into him, if necessary! . . ."

He hurried up the stairs, followed by Hortense and the chief inspector, who was protesting rather peevishly:

"But, I say, look here, it wasn't he who set the place on fire! How do you make out that he set it on fire, seeing that he never left us?"

"Why, he set it on fire beforehand, to be sure!"

"How? I ask you, how?"

"How do I know? But a fire doesn't break out like that, for no reason at all, at the very moment when a man wants to burn compromising papers."

They heard a commotion upstairs. It was the waiters of the restaurant trying to burst the door open. An acrid smell filled the well of the staircase.

Rénine reached the top floor:

"By your leave, friends. I have the key."

He inserted it in the lock and opened the door.

He was met by a gust of smoke so dense that one might well have supposed the whole floor to be ablaze. Rénine at once saw that the fire had gone out of its own accord, for lack of fuel, and that there were no more flames:

"M. Morisseau, you won't let any one come in with us, will you? An intruder might spoil everything. Bolt the door, that will be best."

He stepped into the front room, where the fire had obviously had its chief centre. The furniture, the walls and the ceiling, though blackened by the smoke, had not been touched. As a matter of fact, the fire was confined to a blaze of papers which was still burning in the middle of the room, in front of the window.

Rénine struck his forehead:

"What a fool I am! What an unspeakable ass!"

"Why?" asked the inspector.

"The hat-box, of course! The cardboard hat-box which was standing on the table. That's where he hid the notes. They were there all through our search."

"Impossible!"

"Why, yes, we always overlook that particular hiding-place, the one just under our eyes, within reach of our hands! How could one imagine that a thief would leave sixty thousand francs in an open cardboard box, in which he places his hat when he comes in, with an absent-minded air? That's just the one place we don't look in. . . Well played, M. Dutreuil!"

The inspector, who remained incredulous, repeated:

"No, no, impossible! We were with him and he could not have started the fire himself."

"Everything was prepared beforehand on the supposition that there might be an alarm. . . The hat-box. . . the tissue paper. . . the bank-notes: they must all have been steeped in some inflammable liquid. He must have thrown a match, a chemical preparation or what not into it, as we were leaving."

"But we should have seen him, hang it all! And then is it credible that a man who has committed a murder for the sake of sixty thousand francs should do away with the money in this way? If the hiding-place was such a good one—and it was, because we never discovered it—why this useless destruction?"

"He got frightened, M. Morisseau. Remember that his head is at stake and he knows it. Anything rather than the guillotine; and they—the bank-notes—were the only proof which we had against him. How could he have left them where they were?"

Morisseau was flabbergasted:

"What! The only proof?"

"Why, obviously!"

"But your witnesses? Your evidence? All that you were going to tell the chief?"

"Mere bluff."

"Well, upon my word," growled the bewildered inspector, "you're a cool customer!"

"Would you have taken action without my bluff?"

"No."

"Then what more do you want?"

Rénine stooped to stir the ashes. But there was nothing left, not even those remnants of stiff paper which still retain their shape.

"Nothing," he said. "It's queer, all the same! How the deuce did he manage to set the thing alight?"

He stood up, looking attentively about him. Hortense had a feeling that he was making his supreme effort and that, after this last struggle in the dark, he would either have devised his plan of victory or admit that he was beaten.

Faltering with anxiety, she asked:

"It's all up, isn't it?"

"No, no," he said, thoughtfully, "it's not all up. It was, a few seconds ago. But now there is a gleam of light. . . and one that gives me hope."

"God grant that it may be justified!"

"We must go slowly," he said. "It is only an attempt, but a fine, a very fine attempt; and it may succeed."

He was silent for a moment; then, with an amused smile and a click of the tongue, he said:

"An infernally clever fellow, that Dutreuil! His trick of burning the notes: what a fertile imagination! And what coolness! A pretty dance the beggar has led me! He's a master!"

He fetched a broom from the kitchen and swept a part of the ashes into the next room, returning with a hat-box of the same size and appearance as the one which had been burnt. After crumpling the tissue paper with which it was filled, he placed the hat-box on the little table and set fire to it with a match.

It burst into flames, which he extinguished when they had consumed half the cardboard and nearly all the paper. Then he took from an inner pocket of his waistcoat a bundle of bank-notes and selected six, which he burnt almost completely, arranging the remains and hiding the rest of the notes at the bottom of the box, among the ashes and the blackened bits of paper:

"M. Morisseau," he said, when he had done, "I am asking for your assistance for the last time. Go and fetch Dutreuil. Tell him just this:

'You are unmasked. The notes did not catch fire. Come with me.' And bring him up here."

Despite his hesitation and his fear of exceeding his instructions from the head of the detective service, the chief-inspector was powerless to throw off the ascendancy which Rénine had acquired over him. He left the room.

Rénine turned to Hortense:

"Do you understand my plan of battle?"

"Yes," she said, "but it's a dangerous experiment. Do you think that Dutreuil will fall into the trap?"

"Everything depends on the state of his nerves and the degree of demoralization to which he is reduced. A surprise attack may very well do for him."

"Nevertheless, suppose he recognizes by some sign that the box has been changed?"

"Oh, of course, he has a few chances in his favour! The fellow is much more cunning than I thought and quite capable of wriggling out of the trap. On the other hand, however, how uneasy he must be! How the blood must be buzzing in his ears and obscuring his sight! No, I don't think that he will avoid the trap. . . He will give in. . . He will give in. . ."

They exchanged no more words. Rénine did not move. Hortense was stirred to the very depths of her being. The life of an innocent man hung trembling in the balance. An error of judgment, a little bad luck. . . and, twelve hours later, Jacques Aubrieux would be put to death. And together with a horrible anguish she experienced, in spite of all, a feeling of eager curiosity. What was Prince Rénine going to do? What would be the outcome of the experiment on which he was venturing? What resistance would Gaston Dutreuil offer? She lived through one of those minutes of superhuman tension in which life becomes intensified until it reaches its utmost value.

They heard footsteps on the stairs, the footsteps of men in a hurry. The sound drew nearer. They were reaching the top floor.

Hortense looked at her companion. He had stood up and was listening, his features already transfigured by action. The footsteps were now echoing in the passage. Then, suddenly, he ran to the door and cried:

"Quick! Let's make an end of it!"

Two or three detectives and a couple of waiters entered. He caught hold of Dutreuil in the midst of the detectives and pulled him by the arm, gaily exclaiming:

"Well done, old man! That trick of yours with the table and the water-bottle was really splendid! A masterpiece, on my word! Only, it didn't come off!"

"What do you mean? What's the matter?" mumbled Gaston Dutreuil, staggering.

"What I say: the fire burnt only half the tissue-paper and the hat-box; and, though some of the bank-notes were destroyed, like the tissue-paper, the others are there, at the bottom. . . You understand? The long-sought notes, the great proof of the murder: they're there, where you hid them. . . As chance would have it, they've escaped burning. . . Here, look: there are the numbers; you can check them. . . Oh, you're done for, done for, my beauty!"

The young man drew himself up stiffly. His eyelids quivered. He did not accept Rénine's invitation to look; he examined neither the hat-box nor the bank-notes. From the first moment, without taking the time to reflect and before his instinct could warn him, he believed what he was told and collapsed heavily into a chair, weeping.

The surprise attack, to use Rénine's expression, had succeeded. On seeing all his plans baffled and the enemy master of his secrets, the wretched man had neither the strength nor the perspicacity necessary to defend himself. He threw up the sponge.

Rénine gave him no time to breathe:

"Capital! You're saving your head; and that's all, my good youth! Write down your confession and get it off your chest. Here's a fountain-pen. . . The luck has been against you, I admit. It was devilishly well thought out, your trick of the last moment. You had the bank-notes which were in your way and which you wanted to destroy. Nothing simpler. You take a big, round-bellied water-bottle and stand it on the window-sill. It acts as a burning-glass, concentrating the rays of the sun on the cardboard and tissue-paper, all nicely prepared. Ten minutes later, it bursts into flames. A splendid idea! And, like all great discoveries, it came quite by chance, what? It reminds one of Newton's apple. . . One day, the sun, passing through the water in that bottle, must have set fire to a scrap of cotton or the head of a match; and, as you had the sun at your disposal just now, you said to yourself, 'Now's the time,' and stood the bottle in the right position. My congratulations, Gaston! . . . Look, here's a sheet of paper. Write down: 'It was I who murdered M. Guillaume.' Write, I tell you!"

Leaning over the young man, with all his implacable force of will he compelled him to write, guiding his hand and dictating the sentences. Dutreuil, exhausted, at the end of his strength, wrote as he was told.

"Here's the confession, Mr. Chief-inspector," said Rénine. "You will be good enough to take it to M. Dudouis. These gentlemen," turning to the waiters, from the restaurant, "will, I am sure, consent to serve as witnesses."

And, seeing that Dutreuil, overwhelmed by what had happened, did not move, he gave him a shake:

"Hi, you, look alive! Now that you've been fool enough to confess, make an end of the job, my gentle idiot!"

The other watched him, standing in front of him.

"Obviously," Rénine continued, "you're only a simpleton. The hat-box was fairly burnt to ashes: so were the notes. That hat-box, my dear fellow, is a different one; and those notes belong to me. I even burnt six of them to make you swallow the stunt. And you couldn't make out what had happened. What an owl you must be! To furnish me with evidence at the last moment, when I hadn't a single proof of my own! And such evidence! A written confession! Written before witnesses! . . . Look here, my man, if they do cut off your head—as I sincerely hope they will—upon my word, you'll have jolly well deserved it! Good-bye, Dutreuil!"

Downstairs, in the street, Rénine asked Hortense Daniel to take the car, go to Madeleine Aubrieux and tell her what had happened.

"And you?" asked Hortense.

"I have a lot to do. . . urgent appointments. . ."

"And you deny yourself the pleasure of bringing the good news?"

"It's one of the pleasures that pall upon one. The only pleasure that never flags is that of the fight itself. Afterwards, things cease to be interesting."

She took his hand and for a moment held it in both her own. She would have liked to express all her admiration to that strange man, who seemed to do good as a sort of game and who did it with something like genius. But she was unable to speak. All these rapid incidents had upset her. Emotion constricted her throat and brought the tears to her eyes.

Rénine bowed his head, saying:

"Thank you. I have my reward."

III

The Case of Jean Louis

"Monsieur," continued the young girl, addressing Serge Rénine, "it was while I was spending the Easter holidays at Nice with my father that I made the acquaintance of Jean Louis d'Imbleval. . ."

Rénine interrupted her:

"Excuse me, mademoiselle, but just now you spoke of this young man as Jean Louis Vaurois."

"That's his name also," she said.

"Has he two names then?"

"I don't know. . . I don't know anything about it," she said, with some embarrassment, "and that is why, by Hortense's advice, I came to ask for your help."

This conversation was taking place in Rénine's flat on the Boulevard Haussmann, to which Hortense had brought her friend Geneviève Aymard, a slender, pretty little creature with a face over-shadowed by an expression of the greatest melancholy.

"Rénine will be successful, take my word for it, Geneviève. You will, Rénine, won't you?"

"Please tell me the rest of the story, mademoiselle," he said.

Geneviève continued:

"I was already engaged at the time to a man whom I loathe and detest. My father was trying to force me to marry him and is still trying to do so. Jean Louis and I felt the keenest sympathy for each other, a sympathy that soon developed into a profound and passionate affection which, I can assure you, was equally sincere on both sides. On my return to Paris, Jean Louis, who lives in the country with his mother and his aunt, took rooms in our part of the town; and, as I am allowed to go out by myself, we used to see each other daily. I need not tell you that we were engaged to be married. I told my father so. And this is what he said: 'I don't particularly like the fellow. But, whether it's he or another, what I want is that you should get married. So let him come and ask for your hand. If not, you must do as I say.' In the middle of June, Jean Louis went home to arrange matters with his mother and aunt. I received some passionate letters; and then just these few words:

'There are too many obstacles in the way of our happiness. I give up. I am mad with despair. I love you more than ever. Good-bye and forgive me.'

"Since then, I have received nothing: no reply to my letters and telegrams."

"Perhaps he has fallen in love with somebody else?" asked Rénine. "Or there may be some old connection which he is unable to shake off."

Geneviève shook her head:

"Monsieur, believe me, if our engagement had been broken off for an ordinary reason, I should not have allowed Hortense to trouble you. But it is something quite different, I am absolutely convinced. There's a mystery in Jean Louis' life, or rather an endless number of mysteries which hamper and pursue him. I never saw such distress in a human face; and, from the first moment of our meeting, I was conscious in him of a grief and melancholy which have always persisted, even at times when he was giving himself to our love with the greatest confidence."

"But your impression must have been confirmed by minor details, by things which happened to strike you as peculiar?"

"I don't quite know what to say."

"These two names, for instance?"

"Yes, there was certainly that."

"By what name did he introduce himself to you?"

"Jean Louis d'Imbleval."

"But Jean Louis Vaurois?"

"That's what my father calls him."

"Why?"

"Because that was how he was introduced to my father, at Nice, by a gentleman who knew him. Besides, he carries visiting-cards which describe him under either name."

"Have you never questioned him on this point?"

"Yes, I have, twice. The first time, he said that his aunt's name was Vaurois and his mother's d'Imbleval."

"And the second time?"

"He told me the contrary: he spoke of his mother as Vaurois and of his aunt as d'Imbleval. I pointed this out. He coloured up and I thought it better not to question him any further."

"Does he live far from Paris?"

"Right down in Brittany: at the Manoir d'Elseven, five miles from Carhaix."

Rénine rose and asked the girl, seriously:

"Are you quite certain that he loves you, mademoiselle?"

"I am certain of it and I know too that he represents all my life and all my happiness. He alone can save me. If he can't, then I shall be married in a week's time to a man whom I hate. I have promised my father; and the banns have been published."

"We shall leave for Carhaix, Madame Daniel and I, this evening," said Rénine.

That evening he and Hortense took the train for Brittany. They reached Carhaix at ten o'clock in the morning; and, after lunch, at half past twelve o'clock they stepped into a car borrowed from a leading resident of the district.

"You're looking a little pale, my dear," said Rénine, with a laugh, as they alighted by the gate of the garden at Elseven.

"I'm very fond of Geneviève," she said. "She's the only friend I have. And I'm feeling frightened."

He called her attention to the fact that the central gate was flanked by two wickets bearing the names of Madame d'Imbleval and Madame Vaurois respectively. Each of these wickets opened on a narrow path which ran among the shrubberies of box and aucuba to the left and right of the main avenue. The avenue itself led to an old manor-house, long, low and picturesque, but provided with two clumsily-built, ugly wings, each in a different style of architecture and each forming the destination of one of the side-paths. Madame d'Imbleval evidently lived on the left and Madame Vaurois on the right.

Hortense and Rénine listened. Shrill, hasty voices were disputing inside the house. The sound came through one of the windows of the ground-floor, which was level with the garden and covered throughout its length with red creepers and white roses.

"We can't go any farther," said Hortense. "It would be indiscreet."

"All the more reason," whispered Rénine. "Look here: if we walk straight ahead, we shan't be seen by the people who are quarrelling."

The sounds of conflict were by no means abating; and, when they reached the window next to the front-door, through the roses and creepers they could both see and hear two old ladies shrieking at the tops of their voices and shaking their fists at each other.

The women were standing in the foreground, in a large dining-room where the table was not yet cleared; and at the farther side of the table sat a young man, doubtless Jean Louis himself, smoking his pipe and reading a newspaper, without appearing to trouble about the two old harridans.

One of these, a thin, tall woman, was wearing a purple silk dress; and her hair was dressed in a mass of curls much too yellow for the ravaged face around which they tumbled. The other, who was still thinner, but quite short, was bustling round the room in a cotton dressing-gown and displayed a red, painted face blazing with anger:

"A baggage, that's what you are!" she yelped. "The wickedest woman in the world and a thief into the bargain!"

"I, a thief!" screamed the other.

"What about that business with the ducks at ten francs apiece: don't you call that thieving?"

"Hold your tongue, you low creature! Who stole the fifty-franc note from my dressing-table? Lord, that I should have to live with such a wretch!"

The other started with fury at the outrage and, addressing the young man, cried:

"Jean, are you going to sit there and let me be insulted by your hussy of a d'Imbleval?"

And the tall one retorted, furiously:

"Hussy! Do you hear that, Louis? Look at her, your Vaurois! She's got the airs of a superannuated barmaid! Make her stop, can't you?"

Suddenly Jean Louis banged his fist upon the table, making the plates and dishes jump, and shouted:

"Be quiet, both of you, you old lunatics!"

They turned upon him at once and loaded him with abuse:

"Coward! . . . Hypocrite! . . . Liar! . . . A pretty sort of son you are! . . . The son of a slut and not much better yourself! . . ."

The insults rained down upon him. He stopped his ears with his fingers and writhed as he sat at table like a man who has lost all patience and has need to restrain himself lest he should fall upon his enemy.

Rénine whispered:

"Now's the time to go in."

"In among all those infuriated people?" protested Hortense.

"Exactly. We shall see them better with their masks off."

And, with a determined step, he walked to the door, opened it and entered the room, followed by Hortense.

His advent gave rise to a feeling of stupefaction. The two women stopped yelling, but were still scarlet in the face and trembling with rage. Jean Louis, who was very pale, stood up.

Profiting by the general confusion, Rénine said briskly:

"Allow me to introduce myself. I am Prince Rénine. This is Madame Daniel. We are friends of Mlle. Geneviève Aymard and we have come in her name. I have a letter from her addressed to you, monsieur."

Jean Louis, already disconcerted by the newcomers' arrival, lost countenance entirely on hearing the name of Geneviève. Without quite knowing what he was saying and with the intention of responding to Rénine's courteous behaviour, he tried in his turn to introduce the two ladies and let fall the astounding words:

"My mother, Madame d'Imbleval; my mother, Madame Vaurois."

For some time no one spoke. Rénine bowed. Hortense did not know with whom she should shake hands, with Madame d'Imbleval, the mother, or with Madame Vaurois, the mother. But what happened was that Madame d'Imbleval and Madame Vaurois both at the same time attempted to snatch the letter which Rénine was holding out to Jean Louis, while both at the same time mumbled:

"Mlle. Aymard! . . . She has had the coolness. . . she has had the audacity. . . !"

Then Jean Louis, recovering his self-possession, laid hold of his mother d'Imbleval and pushed her out of the room by a door on the left and next of his mother Vaurois and pushed her out of the room by a door on the right. Then, returning to his two visitors, he opened the envelope and read, in an undertone:

I am to be married in a week, Jean Louis. Come to my rescue, I beseech you. My friend Hortense and Prince Rénine will help you to overcome the obstacles that baffle you. Trust them. I love you.

GENEVIÈVE

He was a rather dull-looking young man, whose very swarthy, lean and bony face certainly bore the expression of melancholy and distress described by Geneviève. Indeed, the marks of suffering were visible in all his harassed features, as well as in his sad and anxious eyes.

He repeated Geneviève's name over and over again, while looking about him with a distracted air. He seemed to be seeking a course of conduct.

He seemed on the point of offering an explanation but could find nothing to say. The sudden intervention had taken him at a disadvantage, like an unforseen attack which he did not know how to meet.

Rénine felt that the adversary would capitulate at the first summons. The man had been fighting so desperately during the last few months and had suffered so severely in the retirement and obstinate silence in which he had taken refuge that he was not thinking of defending himself. Moreover, how could he do so, now that they had forced their way into the privacy of his odious existence?

"Take my word for it, monsieur," declared Rénine, "that it is in your best interests to confide in us. We are Geneviève Aymard's friends. Do not hesitate to speak."

"I can hardly hesitate," he said, "after what you have just heard. This is the life I lead, monsieur. I will tell you the whole secret, so that you may tell it to Geneviève. She will then understand why I have not gone back to her. . . and why I have not the right to do so."

He pushed a chair forward for Hortense. The two men sat down, and, without any need of further persuasion, rather as though he himself felt a certain relief in unburdening himself, he said:

"You must not be surprised, monsieur, if I tell my story with a certain flippancy, for, as a matter of fact, it is a frankly comical story and cannot fail to make you laugh. Fate often amuses itself by playing these imbecile tricks, these monstrous farces which seem as though they must have been invented by the brain of a madman or a drunkard. Judge for yourself. Twenty-seven years ago, the Manoir d'Elseven, which at that time consisted only of the main building, was occupied by an old doctor who, to increase his modest means, used to receive one or two paying guests. In this way, Madame d'Imbleval spent the summer here one year and Madame Vaurois the following summer. Now these two ladies did not know each other. One of them was married to a Breton of a merchant-vessel and the other to a commercial traveller from the Vendée.

"It so happened that they lost their husbands at the same time, at a period when each of them was expecting a baby. And, as they both lived in the country, at places some distance from any town, they wrote to the old doctor that they intended to come to his house for their confinement. . . He agreed. They arrived almost on the same day, in the autumn. Two small bedrooms were prepared for them, behind the room in which we are sitting. The doctor had engaged a nurse, who slept in this very room. Everything was perfectly satisfactory. The ladies were putting the finishing touches to their baby-clothes and were getting on together splendidly. They were determined that their children should be boys and had chosen the names of Jean and Louis respectively. . . One evening the doctor was called out to a case and drove off in his gig with the man-servant, saying that he would not be back till next day. In her master's absence, a little girl who served as maid-of-all-work ran out to keep company with her sweetheart. These accidents destiny turned to account with diabolical malignity. At about midnight, Madame d'Imbleval was seized with the first pains. The nurse, Mlle. Boussignol, had had some training as a midwife and did not lose her head. But, an hour later, Madame Vaurois' turn came; and the tragedy, or I might rather say the tragi-comedy, was enacted amid the screams and moans of the two patients and the bewildered agitation of the nurse running from one to the other, bewailing her fate, opening the window to call out for the doctor or falling on her knees to implore the aid of Providence. . . Madame Vaurois was the first to bring a son into the world. Mlle. Boussignol hurriedly carried him in here, washed and tended him and laid him in the cradle prepared for him. . . But Madame d'Imbleval was screaming with pain; and the nurse had to attend to her while the newborn child was yelling like a stuck pig and the terrified mother, unable to stir from her bed, fainted. . . Add to this all the wretchedness of darkness and disorder, the only lamp, without any oil, for the servant had neglected to fill it, the candles burning out, the moaning of the wind, the screeching of the owls, and you will understand that Mlle. Boussignol was scared out of her wits. However, at five o'clock in the morning, after many tragic incidents, she came in here with the d'Imbleval baby, likewise a boy, washed and tended him, laid him in his cradle and went off to help Madame Vaurois, who had come to herself and was crying out, while Madame d'Imbleval had fainted in her turn. And, when Mlle. Boussignol, having settled the two mothers, but half-crazed with fatigue, her brain in a whirl, returned to the new-born children, she realized with horror that she had wrapped them in similar binders, thrust their feet into similar woolen socks and laid them both, side by side, *in the same cradle*, so that it was impossible to tell Louis d'Imbleval from Jean Vaurois! . . . To make matters worse, when she lifted one of them out of the cradle, she found that his hands were cold as ice and that he had ceased to breathe. He was dead. What was his name and what the survivor's? . . . Three hours later, the doctor found the two women in a condition of frenzied delirium, while the nurse was dragging herself from one bed to the other, entreating the two mothers to forgive her. She held me out first to one, then to the other, to receive their caresses—for I was the surviving child—and they first kissed me and then pushed me away; for, after all, who was I? The son of the widowed Madame d'Imbleval and the late merchant-captain or the son of the widowed Madame Vaurois and the late commercial traveller? There was not a clue by which they could tell. . . The doctor begged each of the two mothers to sacrifice her rights, at least from the legal point of view, so that I might be called either Louis d'Imbleval or Jean Vaurois. They refused absolutely. 'Why Jean Vaurois, if he's a d'Imbleval?' protested the one. 'Why Louis d'Imbleval, if he's a Vaurois?' retorted the other. And I was registered under the name of Jean Louis, the son of an unknown father and mother."

Prince Rénine had listened in silence. But Hortense, as the story approached its conclusion, had given way to a hilarity which she could no longer restrain and suddenly, in spite of all her efforts, she burst into a fit of the wildest laughter:

"Forgive me," she said, her eyes filled with tears, "do forgive me; it's too much for my nerves. . ."

"Don't apologize, madame," said the young man, gently, in a voice free from resentment. "I warned you that my story was laughable; I, better than any one, know how absurd, how nonsensical it is. Yes, the whole thing is perfectly grotesque. But believe me when I tell you that it was no fun in reality. It seems a humorous situation and it remains humorous by the force of circumstances; but it is also horrible. You can see that for yourself, can't you? The two mothers, neither of whom was certain of being a mother, but neither of whom was certain that she was not one, both clung to Jean Louis. He might be a stranger; on the other hand, he might be their own flesh and blood. They loved him to excess and fought for him furiously. And, above all, they both came to hate each other with a deadly hatred. Differing completely in character and education and obliged to live together because neither was willing to forego the advantage of her possible maternity, they lived the life of irreconcilable enemies who can never lay their weapons aside. . . I

MAURICE LEBLANC

grew up in the midst of this hatred and had it instilled into me by both of them. When my childish heart, hungering for affection, inclined me to one of them, the other would seek to inspire me with loathing and contempt for her. In this manor-house, which they bought on the old doctor's death and to which they added the two wings, I was the involuntary torturer and their daily victim. Tormented as a child, and, as a young man, leading the most hideous of lives, I doubt if any one on earth ever suffered more than I did."

"You ought to have left them!" exclaimed Hortense, who had stopped laughing.

"One can't leave one's mother; and one of those two women was my mother. And a woman can't abandon her son; and each of them was entitled to believe that I was her son. We were all three chained together like convicts, with chains of sorrow, compassion, doubt and also of hope that the truth might one day become apparent. And here we still are, all three, insulting one another and blaming one another for our wasted lives. Oh, what a hell! And there was no escaping it. I tried often enough. . . but in vain. The broken bonds became tied again. Only this summer, under the stimulus of my love for Geneviève, I tried to free myself and did my utmost to persuade the two women whom I call mother. And then. . . and then! I was up against their complaints, their immediate hatred of the wife, of the stranger, whom I was proposing to force upon them. . . I gave way. What sort of a life would Geneviève have had here, between Madame d'Imbleval and Madame Vaurois? I had no right to victimize her."

Jean Louis, who had been gradually becoming excited, uttered these last words in a firm voice, as though he would have wished his conduct to be ascribed to conscientious motives and a sense of duty. In reality, as Rénine and Hortense clearly saw, his was an unusually weak nature, incapable of reacting against a ridiculous position from which he had suffered ever since he was a child and which he had come to look upon as final and irremediable. He endured it as a man bears a cross which he has no right to cast aside; and at the same time he was ashamed of it. He had never spoken of it to Geneviève, from dread of ridicule; and afterwards, on returning to his prison, he had remained there out of habit and weakness.

He sat down to a writing-table and quickly wrote a letter which he handed to Rénine:

"Would you be kind enough to give this note to Mlle. Aymard and beg her once more to forgive me?"

Rénine did not move and, when the other pressed the letter upon him, he took it and tore it up.

"What does this mean?" asked the young man.

"It means that I will not charge myself with any message."

"Why?"

"Because you are coming with us."

"I?"

"Yes. You will see Mlle. Aymard to-morrow and ask for her hand in marriage."

Jean Louis looked at Rénine with a rather disdainful air, as though he were thinking:

"Here's a man who has not understood a word of what I've been explaining to him."

But Hortense went up to Rénine:

"Why do you say that?"

"Because it will be as I say."

"But you must have your reasons?"

"One only; but it will be enough, provided this gentleman is so kind as to help me in my enquiries."

"Enquiries? With what object?" asked the young man.

"With the object of proving that your story is not quite accurate."

Jean Louis took umbrage at this:

"I must ask you to believe, monsieur, that I have not said a word which is not the exact truth."

"I expressed myself badly," said Rénine, with great kindliness. "Certainly you have not said a word that does not agree with what you believe to be the exact truth. But the truth is not, cannot be what you believe it to be."

The young man folded his arms:

"In any case, monsieur, it seems likely that I should know the truth better than you do."

"Why better? What happened on that tragic night can obviously be known to you only at secondhand. You have no proofs. Neither have Madame d'Imbleval and Madame Vaurois."

"No proofs of what?" exclaimed Jean Louis, losing patience.

"No proofs of the confusion that took place."

"What! Why, it's an absolute certainty! The two children were laid in the same cradle, with no marks to distinguish one from the other; and the nurse was unable to tell. . ."

"At least, that's her version of it," interrupted Rénine.

"What's that? Her version? But you're accusing the woman."

"I'm accusing her of nothing."

"Yes, you are: you're accusing her of lying. And why should she lie? She had no interest in doing so; and her tears and despair are so much evidence of her good faith. For, after all, the two mothers were there. . . they saw the woman weeping. . . they questioned her. . . And then, I repeat, what interest had she. . . ?"

Jean Louis was greatly excited. Close beside him, Madame d'Imbleval and Madame Vaurois, who had no doubt been listening behind the doors and who had stealthily entered the room, stood stammering, in amazement:

"No, no. . . it's impossible. . . We've questioned her over and over again. Why should she tell a lie? . . ."

"Speak, monsieur, speak," Jean Louis enjoined. "Explain yourself. Give your reasons for trying to cast doubt upon an absolute truth!"

"Because that truth is inadmissible," declared Rénine, raising his voice and growing excited in turn to the point of punctuating his remarks by thumping the table. "No, things don't happen like that. No, fate does not display those refinements of cruelty and chance is not added to chance with such reckless extravagance! It was already an unprecedented chance that, on the very night on which the doctor, his man-servant and his maid were out of the house, the two ladies should be seized with labour-pains at the same hour and should bring two sons into the world at the same time. Don't let us add a still more exceptional event! Enough of the uncanny! Enough of lamps that go out and candles that refuse to burn! No and again no, it is not admissable that a midwife should become confused in the essential details of her trade. However bewildered she may be by the unforeseen nature of the circumstances, a remnant of instinct is still on the alert, so that there is a place prepared for each child and each is kept distinct from the other. The first child is here, the second is there. Even if they are lying side by side, one is on the left and the other on the right. Even if they are wrapped in the same kind of binders, some little detail differs, a trifle which is recorded by the memory and which is inevitably recalled to the mind without any need of reflection. Confusion? I refuse to believe in it. Impossible to tell one from the other? It isn't true. In the world of fiction, yes, one can imagine all sorts of fantastic accidents and heap contradiction on contradiction. But, in the world of reality, at the very heart of reality, there is always a fixed point, a solid nucleus, about which the facts group themselves in accordance with a logical order. I therefore declare most positively that Nurse Boussignol could not have mixed up the two children."

All this he said decisively, as though he had been present during the night in question; and so great was his power of persuasion that from the very first he shook the certainty of those who for more than a quarter of a century had never doubted.

The two women and their son pressed round him and questioned him with breathless anxiety:

"Then you think that she may know. . . that she may be able to tell us. . . ?"

He corrected himself:

"I don't say yes and I don't say no. All I say is that there was something in her behaviour during those hours that does not tally with her statements and with reality. All the vast and intolerable mystery that has weighed down upon you three arises not from a momentary lack of attention but from something of which we do not know, but of which she does. That is what I maintain; and that is what happened."

Jean Louis said, in a husky voice:

"She is alive. . . She lives at Carhaix. . . We can send for her. . ."

Hortense at once proposed:

"Would you like me to go for her? I will take the motor and bring her back with me. Where does she live?"

"In the middle of the town, at a little draper's shop. The chauffeur will show you. Mlle. Boussignol: everybody knows her. . ."

"And, whatever you do," added Rénine, "don't warn her in any way. If she's uneasy, so much the better. But don't let her know what we want with her."

Twenty minutes passed in absolute silence. Rénine paced the room, in which the fine old furniture, the handsome tapestries, the well-bound books and pretty knick-knacks denoted a love of art and a seeking after style in Jean Louis. This room was really his. In the adjoining apartments on either side, through the open doors, Rénine was able to note the bad taste of the two mothers.

He went up to Jean Louis and, in a low voice, asked:

"Are they well off?"

"Yes."

"And you?"

"They settled the manor-house upon me, with all the land around it, which makes me quite independent."

"Have they any relations?"

"Sisters, both of them."

"With whom they could go to live?"

"Yes; and they have sometimes thought of doing so. But there can't be any question of that. Once more, I assure you. . ."

Meantime the car had returned. The two women jumped up hurriedly, ready to speak.

"Leave it to me," said Rénine, "and don't be surprised by anything that I say. It's not a matter of asking her questions but of frightening her, of flurrying her. . . The sudden attack," he added between his teeth.

The car drove round the lawn and drew up outside the windows. Hortense sprang out and helped an old woman to alight, dressed in a fluted linen cap, a black velvet bodice and a heavy gathered skirt.

The old woman entered in a great state of alarm. She had a pointed face, like a weasel's, with a prominent mouth full of protruding teeth.

"What's the matter, Madame d'Imbleval?" she asked, timidly stepping into the room from which the doctor had once driven her. "Good day to you, Madame Vaurois."

The ladies did not reply. Rénine came forward and said, sternly:

"Mlle. Boussignol, I have been sent by the Paris police to throw light upon a tragedy which took place here twenty-seven years ago. I have just secured evidence that you have distorted the truth and that, as the result of your false declarations, the birth-certificate of one of the children born in the course of that night is inaccurate. Now false declarations in matters of birth-certificates are misdemeanours punishable by law. I shall therefore be obliged to take you to Paris to be interrogated. . . unless you are prepared here and now to confess everything that might repair the consequences of your offence."

The old maid was shaking in every limb. Her teeth were chattering. She was evidently incapable of opposing the least resistance to Rénine.

"Are you ready to confess everything?" he asked.

"Yes," she panted.

"Without delay? I have to catch a train. The business must be settled immediately. If you show the least hesitation, I take you with me. Have you made up your mind to speak?"

"Yes."

He pointed to Jean Louis:

"Whose son is this gentleman? Madame d'Imbleval's?"

"No."

"Madame Vaurois', therefore?"

"No."

A stupefied silence welcomed the two replies.

"Explain yourself," Rénine commanded, looking at his watch.

Then Madame Boussignol fell on her knees and said, in so low and dull a voice that they had to bend over her in order to catch the sense of what she was mumbling:

"Some one came in the evening. . . a gentleman with a new-born baby wrapped in blankets, which he wanted the doctor to look after. As the doctor wasn't there, he waited all night and it was he who did it all."

"Did what?" asked Rénine. "What did he do? What happened?"

"Well, what happened was that it was not one child but the two of them that died: Madame d'Imbleval's and Madame Vaurois' too, both in convulsions. Then the gentleman, seeing this, said, 'This shows me where my duty lies. I must seize this opportunity of making sure that my own boy shall be happy and well cared for. Put him in the place of one of the dead children.' He offered me a big sum of money, saying that this one payment would save him the expense of providing for his child every month; and I accepted. Only, I did not know in whose place to put him and whether to say that the boy was Louis d'Imbleval or Jean Vaurois. The gentleman thought a moment and said neither. Then he explained to me what I was to do and what I was to say after he had gone. And, while I was dressing his boy in vest and binders the same as one of the dead children, he wrapped the other in the blankets he had brought with him and went out into the night."

Mlle. Boussignol bent her head and wept. After a moment, Rénine said:

"Your deposition agrees with the result of my investigations."

"Can I go?"

"Yes."

"And is it over, as far as I'm concerned? They won't be talking about this all over the district?"

"No. Oh, just one more question: do you know the man's name?"

"No. He didn't tell me his name."

"Have you ever seen him since?"

"Never."

"Have you anything more to say?"

　　　　　　　　　　　　　　　　　　　　　　MAURICE LEBLANC

"No."

"Are you prepared to sign the written text of your confession?"

"Yes."

"Very well. I shall send for you in a week or two. Till then, not a word to anybody."

He saw her to the door and closed it after her. When he returned, Jean Louis was between the two old ladies and all three were holding hands. The bond of hatred and wretchedness which had bound them had suddenly snapped; and this rupture, without requiring them to reflect upon the matter, filled them with a gentle tranquillity of which they were hardly conscious, but which made them serious and thoughtful.

"Let's rush things," said Rénine to Hortense. "This is the decisive moment of the battle. We must get Jean Louis on board."

Hortense seemed preoccupied. She whispered:

"Why did you let the woman go? Were you satisfied with her statement?"

"I don't need to be satisfied. She told us what happened. What more do you want?"

"Nothing. . . I don't know. . ."

"We'll talk about it later, my dear. For the moment, I repeat, we must get Jean Louis on board. And immediately. . . Otherwise. . ."

He turned to the young man:

"You agree with me, don't you, that, things being as they are, it is best for you and Madame Vaurois and Madame d'Imbleval to separate for a time? That will enable you all to see matters more clearly and to decide in perfect freedom what is to be done. Come with us, monsieur. The most pressing thing is to save Geneviève Aymard, your *fiancée*."

Jean Louis stood perplexed and undecided. Rénine turned to the two women:

"That is your opinion too, I am sure, ladies?"

They nodded.

"You see, monsieur," he said to Jean Louis, "we are all agreed. In great crises, there is nothing like separation. . . a few days' respite. Quickly now, monsieur."

And, without giving him time to hesitate, he drove him towards his bedroom to pack up.

Half an hour later, Jean Louis left the manor-house with his new friends.

"And he won't go back until he's married," said Rénine to Hortense, as they were waiting at Carhaix station, to which the car had taken them, while Jean Louis was attending to his luggage. "Everything's for the best. Are you satisfied?"

"Yes, Geneviève will be glad," she replied, absently.

When they had taken their seats in the train, Rénine and she repaired to the dining-car. Rénine, who had asked Hortense several questions to which she had replied only in monosyllables, protested:

"What's the matter with you, my child? You look worried!"

"I? Not at all!"

"Yes, yes, I know you. Now, no secrets, no mysteries!"

She smiled:

"Well, since you insist on knowing if I am satisfied, I am bound to admit that of course I am. . . as regards my friend Geneviève, but that, in another respect—from the point of view of the adventure—I have an uncomfortable sort of feeling. . ."

"To speak frankly, I haven't 'staggered' you this time?"

"Not very much."

"I seem to you to have played a secondary part. For, after all, what have I done? We arrived. We listened to Jean Louis' tale of woe. I had a midwife fetched. And that was all."

"Exactly. I want to know if that *was* all; and I'm not quite sure. To tell you the truth, our other adventures left behind them an impression which was—how shall I put it?—more definite, clearer."

"And this one strikes you as obscure?"

"Obscure, yes, and incomplete."

"But in what way?"

"I don't know. Perhaps it has something to do with that woman's confession. Yes, very likely that is it. It was all so unexpected and so short."

"Well, of course, I cut it short, as you can readily imagine!" said Rénine, laughing. "We didn't want too many explanations."

"What do you mean?"

"Why, if she had given her explanations with too much detail, we should have ended by doubting what she was telling us."

"By doubting it?"

"Well, hang it all, the story is a trifle far-fetched! That fellow arriving at night, with a live baby in his pocket, and going away with a dead one: the thing hardly holds water. But you see, my dear, I hadn't much time to coach the unfortunate woman in her part."

Hortense stared at him in amazement:

"What on earth do you mean?"

"Well, you know how dull-witted these countrywomen are. And she and I had no time to spare. So we worked out a little scene in a hurry. . . and she really didn't act it so badly. It was all in the right key: terror, *tremolo*, tears. . ."

"Is it possible?" murmured Hortense. "Is it possible? You had seen her beforehand?"

"I had to, of course."

"But when?"

"This morning, when we arrived. While you were titivating yourself at the hotel at Carhaix, I was running round to see what information I could pick up. As you may imagine, everybody in the district knows the d'Imbleval-Vaurois story. I was at once directed to the former midwife, Mlle. Boussignol. With Mlle. Boussignol it did not take long. Three minutes to settle a new version of what had happened and ten thousand francs to induce her to repeat that. . . more or less credible. . . version to the people at the manor-house."

"A quite incredible version!"

"Not so bad as all that, my child, seeing that you believed it. . . and the others too. And that was the essential thing. What I had to do was to demolish at one blow a truth which had been twenty-seven years in existence and which was all the more firmly established because it was founded on actual facts. That was why I went for it with all my might and attacked it by sheer force of eloquence. Impossible to identify the children? I deny it. Inevitable confusion? It's not true. 'You're all three,' I say, 'the victims of something which I don't know but which it is your duty to clear up!' 'That's easily done,' says Jean Louis, whose conviction is at once shaken. 'Let's send for Mlle. Boussignol.' 'Right! Let's send for her.' Whereupon Mlle. Boussignol arrives and mumbles out the little speech which I have taught her. Sensation! General stupefaction. . . of which I take advantage to carry off our young man!"

Hortense shook her head:

"But they'll get over it, all three of them, on thinking!"

"Never! Never! They will have their doubts, perhaps. But they will never consent to feel certain! They will never agree to think! Use your imagination! Here are three people whom I have rescued from the hell in which they have been floundering for a quarter of a century. Do you think they're going back to it? Here are three people who, from weakness or a false sense of duty, had not the courage to escape. Do you think that they won't cling like grim death to the liberty which I'm giving them? Nonsense! Why, they would have swallowed a hoax twice as difficult to digest as that which Mlle. Boussignol dished up for them! After all, my version was no more absurd than the truth. On the contrary. And they swallowed it whole! Look at this: before we left, I heard Madame d'Imbleval and Madame Vaurois speak of an immediate removal. They were already becoming quite affectionate at the thought of seeing the last of each other."

"But what about Jean Louis?"

"Jean Louis? Why, he was fed up with his two mothers! By Jingo, one can't do with two mothers in a life-time! What a situation! And when one has the luck to be able to choose between having two mothers or none at all, why, bless me, one doesn't hesitate! And, besides, Jean Louis is in love with Geneviève." He laughed. "And he loves her well enough, I hope and trust, not to inflict two mothers-in-law upon her! Come, you may be easy in your mind. Your friend's happiness is assured; and that is all you asked for. All that matters is the object which we achieve and not the more or less peculiar nature of the methods which we employ. And, if some adventures are wound up and some mysteries elucidated by looking for and finding cigarette-ends, or incendiary water-bottles and blazing hat-boxes as on our last expedition, others call for psychology and for purely psychological solutions. I have spoken. And I charge you to be silent."

"Silent?"

"Yes, there's a man and woman sitting behind us who seem to be saying something uncommonly interesting."

"But they're talking in whispers."

"Just so. When people talk in whispers, it's always about something shady."

He lit a cigarette and sat back in his chair. Hortense listened, but in vain. As for him, he was emitting little slow puffs of smoke.

Fifteen minutes later, the train stopped and the man and woman got out.

"Pity," said Rénine, "that I don't know their names or where they're going. But I know where to find them. My dear, we have a new adventure before us."

Hortense protested:

"Oh, no, please, not yet! . . . Give me a little rest! . . . And oughtn't we to think of Geneviève?"

He seemed greatly surprised:

"Why, all that's over and done with! Do you mean to say you want to waste any more time over that old story? Well, I for my part confess that I've lost all interest in the man with the two mammas."

And this was said in such a comical tone and with such diverting sincerity that Hortense was once more seized with a fit of giggling. Laughter alone was able to relax her exasperated nerves and to distract her from so many contradictory emotions.

IV

The Tell-Tale Film

D o look at the man who's playing the butler," said Serge Rénine.
"What is there peculiar about him?" asked Hortense.

They were sitting in the balcony at a picture-palace, to which Hortense had asked to be taken so that she might see on the screen the daughter of a lady, now dead, who used to give her piano-lessons. Rose Andrée, a lovely girl with lissome movements and a smiling face, was that evening figuring in a new film, *The Happy Princess*, which she lit up with her high spirits and her warm, glowing beauty.

Rénine made no direct reply, but, during a pause in the performance, continued:

"I sometimes console myself for an indifferent film by watching the subordinate characters. It seems to me that those poor devils, who are made to rehearse certain scenes ten or twenty times over, must often be thinking of other things than their parts at the time of the final exposure. And it's great fun noting those little moments of distraction which reveal something of their temperament, of their instinct self. As, for instance, in the case of that butler: look!"

The screen now showed a luxuriously served table. The Happy Princess sat at the head, surrounded by all her suitors. Half-a-dozen footmen moved about the room, under the orders of the butler, a big fellow with a dull, coarse face, a common appearance and a pair of enormous eyebrows which met across his forehead in a single line.

"He looks a brute," said Hortense, "but what do you see in him that's peculiar?"

"Just note how he gazes at the princess and tell me if he doesn't stare at her oftener than he ought to."

"I really haven't noticed anything, so far," said Hortense.

"Why, of course he does!" Serge Rénine declared. "It is quite obvious that in actual life he entertains for Rose Andrée personal feelings which are quite out of place in a nameless servant. It is possible that, in real life, no one has any idea of such a thing; but, on the screen, when he is not watching himself, or when he thinks that the actors at rehearsal cannot see him, his secret escapes him. Look. . ."

The man was standing still. It was the end of dinner. The princess was drinking a glass of champagne and he was gloating over her with his glittering eyes half-hidden behind their heavy lids.

Twice again they surprised in his face those strange expressions to which Rénine ascribed an emotional meaning which Hortense refused to see:

"It's just his way of looking at people," she said.

The first part of the film ended. There were two parts, divided by an *entr'acte*. The notice on the programme stated that "a year had elapsed and that the Happy Princess was living in a pretty Norman cottage, all hung with creepers, together with her husband, a poor musician."

The princess was still happy, as was evident on the screen, still as attractive as ever and still besieged by the greatest variety of suitors. Nobles and commoners, peasants and financiers, men of all kinds fell swooning at her feet; and prominent among them was a sort of boorish solitary, a shaggy, half-wild woodcutter, whom she met whenever she went out for a walk. Armed with his axe, a formidable, crafty being, he prowled around the cottage; and the spectators felt with a sense of dismay that a peril was hanging over the Happy Princess' head.

"Look at that!" whispered Rénine. "Do you realise who the man of the woods is?"

"No."

"Simply the butler. The same actor is doubling the two parts."

In fact, notwithstanding the new figure which he cut, the butler's movements and postures were apparent under the heavy gait and rounded shoulders of the woodcutter, even as under the unkempt beard and long, thick hair the once clean-shaven face was visible with the cruel expression and the bushy line of the eyebrows.

The princess, in the background, was seen to emerge from the thatched cottage. The man hid himself behind a clump of trees. From time to time, the screen displayed, on an enormously enlarged scale, his fiercely rolling eyes or his murderous hands with their huge thumbs.

"The man frightens me," said Hortense. "He is really terrifying."

"Because he's acting on his own account," said Rénine. "You must understand that, in the space of three or four months that appears to separate the dates at which the two films were made, his passion has made progress; and to him it is not the princess who is coming but Rose Andrée."

The man crouched low. The victim approached, gaily and unsuspectingly. She passed, heard a sound, stopped and looked about her with a smiling air which became attentive, then uneasy, and then more and more anxious. The woodcutter had pushed aside the branches and was coming through the copse.

They were now standing face to face. He opened his arms as though to seize her. She tried to scream, to call out for help; but the arms closed around her before she could offer the slightest resistance. Then he threw her over his shoulder and began to run.

"Are you satisfied?" whispered Rénine. "Do you think that this fourth-rate actor would have had all that strength and energy if it had been any other woman than Rose Andrée?"

Meanwhile the woodcutter was crossing the skirt of a forest and plunging through great trees and masses of rocks. After setting the princess down, he cleared the entrance to a cave which the daylight entered by a slanting crevice.

A succession of views displayed the husband's despair, the search and the discovery of some small branches which had been broken by the princess and which showed the path that had been taken. Then came the final scene, with the terrible struggle between the man and the woman when the woman, vanquished and exhausted, is flung to the ground, the sudden arrival of the husband and the shot that puts an end to the brute's life. . .

"WELL," SAID RÉNINE, WHEN THEY had left the picture-palace—and he spoke with a certain gravity—"I maintain that the daughter of your old piano-teacher has been in danger ever since the day when that last scene was filmed. I maintain that this scene represents not so much an assault by the man of the woods on the Happy Princess as a violent and frantic attack by an actor on the woman he desires. Certainly it all happened within the bounds prescribed by the part and nobody saw anything in it—nobody except perhaps Rose Andrée herself—but I, for my part, have detected flashes of passion which leave not a doubt in my mind. I have seen glances that betrayed the wish and even the intention to commit murder. I have seen clenched hands, ready to strangle, in short, a score of details which prove to me that, at that time, the man's instinct was urging him to kill the woman who could never be his."

"And it all amounts to what?"

"We must protect Rose Andrée if she is still in danger and if it is not too late."

"And to do this?"

"We must get hold of further information."

"From whom?"

"From the World's Cinema Company, which made the film. I will go to them to-morrow morning. Will you wait for me in your flat about lunch-time?"

At heart, Hortense was still sceptical. All these manifestations of passion, of which she denied neither the ardour nor the ferocity, seemed to her to be the rational behaviour of a good actor. She had seen nothing of the terrible tragedy which Rénine contended that he had divined; and she wondered whether he was not erring through an excess of imagination.

"Well," she asked, next day, not without a touch of irony, "how far have you got? Have you made a good bag? Anything mysterious? Anything thrilling?"

"Pretty good."

"Oh, really? And your so-called lover. . ."

"Is one Dalbrèque, originally a scene-painter, who played the butler in the first part of the film and the man of the woods in the second and was so much appreciated that they engaged him for a new film. Consequently, he has been acting lately. He was acting near Paris. But, on the morning of Friday the 18th of September, he broke into the garage of the World's Cinema Company and made off with a magnificent car and forty thousand francs in money. Information was lodged with the police; and on the Sunday the car was found a little way outside Dreux. And up to now the enquiry has revealed two things, which will appear in the papers to-morrow: first, Dalbrèque is alleged to have committed a murder which created a great stir last year, the murder of Bourguet, the jeweller; secondly, on the day after his two robberies, Dalbrèque was driving through Le Havre in a motor-car with two men who helped him to carry off, in broad daylight and in a crowded street, a lady whose identity has not yet been discovered."

"Rose Andrée?" asked Hortense, uneasily.

"I have just been to Rose Andrée's: the World's Cinema Company gave me her address. Rose Andrée spent this summer travelling and then stayed for a fortnight in the Seine-inférieure, where she has a small place of her own, the actual cottage in *The Happy Princess*. On receiving an invitation from America to do a film there, she came back to Paris, registered her luggage at the Gare Saint-Lazare and left on Friday the 18th of September, intending to sleep at Le Havre and take Saturday's boat."

"Friday the 18th," muttered Hortense, "the same day on which that man. . ."

"And it was on the Saturday that a woman was carried off by him at Le Havre. I looked in at the Compagnie Transatlantique and a brief investigation showed that Rose Andrée had booked a cabin but that the cabin remained unoccupied. The passenger did not turn up."

"This is frightful. She has been carried off. You were right."

"I fear so."

"What have you decided to do?"

"Adolphe, my chauffeur, is outside with the car. Let us go to Le Havre. Up to the present, Rose Andrée's disappearance does not seem to have become known. Before it does and before the police identify the woman carried off by Dalbrèque with the woman who did not turn up to claim her cabin, we will get on Rose Andrée's track."

There was not much said on the journey. At four o'clock Hortense and Rénine reached Rouen. But here Rénine changed his road.

"Adolphe, take the left bank of the Seine."

He unfolded a motoring-map on his knees and, tracing the route with his finger, showed Hortense that, if you draw a line from Le Havre, or rather from Quillebeuf, where the road crosses the Seine, to Dreux, where the stolen car was found, this line passes through Routot, a market-town lying west of the forest of Brotonne:

"Now it was in the forest of Brotonne," he continued, "according to what I heard, that the second part of *The Happy Princess* was filmed. And the question that arises is this: having got hold of Rose Andrée, would it not occur to Dalbrèque, when passing near the forest on the Saturday night, to hide his prey there, while his two accomplices went on to Dreux and from there returned to Paris? The cave was quite near. Was he not bound to go to it? How should he do otherwise? Wasn't it while running to this cave, a few months ago, that he held in his arms, against his breast, within reach of his lips, the woman whom he loved and whom he has now conquered? By every rule of fate and logic, the adventure is being repeated all over again. . . but this time in reality. Rose Andrée is a captive. There is no hope of rescue. The forest is vast and lonely. That night, or on one of the following nights, Rose Andrée must surrender. . . or die."

Hortense gave a shudder:

"We shall be too late. Besides, you don't suppose that he's keeping her a prisoner?"

"Certainly not. The place I have in mind is at a cross-roads and is not a safe retreat. But we may discover some clue or other."

The shades of night were falling from the tall trees when they entered the ancient forest of Brotonne, full of Roman remains and mediaeval relics. Rénine knew the forest well and remembered that near a famous oak, known as the Wine-cask, there was a cave which must be the cave of the Happy Princess. He found it easily, switched on his electric torch, rummaged in the dark corners and brought Hortense back to the entrance:

"There's nothing inside," he said, "but here is the evidence which I was looking for. Dalbrèque was obsessed by the recollection of the film, but so was Rose Andrée. The Happy Princess had broken off the tips of the branches on the way through the forest. Rose Andrée has managed to break off some to the right of this opening, in the hope that she would be discovered as on the first occasion."

"Yes," said Hortense, "it's a proof that she has been here; but the proof is three weeks old. Since that time. . ."

"Since that time, she is either dead and buried under a heap of leaves or else alive in some hole even lonelier than this."

"If so, where is he?"

Rénine pricked up his ears. Repeated blows of the axe were sounding from some distance, no doubt coming from a part of the forest that was being cleared.

"He?" said Rénine, "I wonder whether he may not have continued to behave under the influence of the film and whether the man of the woods in *The Happy Princess* has not quite naturally resumed his calling. For how is the man to live, to obtain his food, without attracting attention? He will have found a job."

"We can't make sure of that."

"We might, by questioning the woodcutters whom we can hear."

The car took them by a forest-road to another cross-roads where they entered on foot a track which was deeply rutted by waggon-wheels. The sound of axes ceased. After walking for a quarter of an hour, they met a dozen men who, having finished work for the day, were returning to the villages near by.

"Will this path take us to Routot?" ask Rénine, in order to open a conversation with them.

"No, you're turning your backs on it," said one of the men, gruffly.

And he went on, accompanied by his mates.

Hortense and Rénine stood rooted to the spot. They had recognized the butler. His cheeks and chin were shaved, but his upper lip was covered by a black moustache, evidently dyed. The eyebrows no longer met and were reduced to normal dimensions.

Thus, in less than twenty hours, acting on the vague hints supplied by the bearing of a film-actor, Serge Rénine had touched the very heart of the tragedy by means of purely psychological arguments.

"Rose Andrée is alive," he said. "Otherwise Dalbrèque would have left the country. The poor thing must be imprisoned and bound up; and he takes her some food at night."

"We will save her, won't we?"

"Certainly, by keeping a watch on him and, if necessary, but in the last resort, compelling him by force to give up his secret."

They followed the woodcutter at a distance and, on the pretext that the car needed overhauling, engaged rooms in the principal inn at Routot.

Attached to the inn was a small café from which they were separated by the entrance to the yard and above which were two rooms, reached by a wooden outer staircase, at one side. Dalbrèque occupied one of these rooms and Rénine took the other for his chauffeur.

Next morning he learnt from Adolphe that Dalbrèque, on the previous evening, after all the lights were out, had carried down a bicycle from his room and mounted it and had not returned until shortly before sunrise.

The bicycle tracks led Rénine to the uninhabited Château des Landes, five miles from the village. They disappeared in a rocky path which ran beside the park down to the Seine, opposite the Jumièges peninsula.

Next night, he took up his position there. At eleven o'clock, Dalbrèque climbed a bank, scrambled over a wire fence, hid his bicycle under the branches and moved away. It seemed impossible to follow him in the pitchy darkness, on a mossy soil that muffled the sound of footsteps. Rénine did not make the attempt; but, at daybreak, he came with his chauffeur and hunted through the park all the morning. Though the park, which covered the side of a hill and was bounded below by the river, was not very large, he found no clue which gave him any reason to suppose that Rose Andrée was imprisoned there.

He therefore went back to the village, with the firm intention of taking action that evening and employing force:

"This state of things cannot go on," he said to Hortense. "I must rescue Rose Andrée at all costs and save her from that ruffian's clutches. He must be made to speak. He must. Otherwise there's a danger that we may be too late."

That day was Sunday; and Dalbrèque did not go to work. He did not leave his room except for lunch and went upstairs again immediately afterwards. But at three o'clock Rénine and Hortense, who were keeping a watch on him from the inn, saw him come down the wooden staircase, with his bicycle on his shoulder. Leaning it against the bottom step, he inflated the tires and fastened to the handle-bar a rather bulky object wrapped in a newspaper.

"By Jove!" muttered Rénine.

"What's the matter?"

In front of the café was a small terrace bordered on the right and left by spindle-trees planted in boxes, which were connected by a paling. Behind the shrubs, sitting on a bank but stooping forward so that they could see Dalbrèque through the branches, were four men.

"Police!" said Rénine. "What bad luck! If those fellows take a hand, they will spoil everything."

"Why? On the contrary, I should have thought. . ."

"Yes, they will. They will put Dalbrèque out of the way. . . and then? Will that give us Rose Andrée?"

Dalbrèque had finished his preparations. Just as he was mounting his bicycle, the detectives rose in a body, ready to make a dash for him. But Dalbrèque, though quite unconscious of their presence, changed his mind and went back to his room as though he had forgotten something.

"Now's the time!" said Rénine. "I'm going to risk it. But it's a difficult situation and I've no great hopes."

He went out into the yard and, at a moment when the detectives were not looking, ran up the staircase, as was only natural if he wished to give an order to his chauffeur. But he had no sooner reached the rustic balcony at the back of the house, which gave admission to the two bedrooms than he stopped. Dalbrèque's door was open. Rénine walked in.

Dalbrèque stepped back, at once assuming the defensive:

"What do you want? Who said you could. . ."

"Silence!" whispered Rénine, with an imperious gesture. "It's all up with you!"

"What are you talking about?" growled the man, angrily.

"Lean out of your window. There are four men below on the watch for you to leave, four detectives."

Dalbrèque leant over the terrace and muttered an oath:

"On the watch for me?" he said, turning round. "What do I care?"

"They have a warrant."

He folded his arms:

"Shut up with your piffle! A warrant! What's that to me?"

"Listen," said Rénine, "and let us waste no time. It's urgent. Your name's Dalbrèque, or, at least, that's the name under which you acted in *The Happy Princess* and under which the police are looking for you as being the murderer of Bourguet the jeweller, the man who stole a motor-car and forty thousand francs from the World's Cinema Company and the man who abducted a woman at Le Havre. All this is known and proved. . . and here's the upshot. Four men downstairs. Myself here, my chauffeur in the next room. You're done for. Do you want me to save you?"

Dalbrèque gave his adversary a long look:

"Who are you?"

"A friend of Rose Andrée's," said Rénine.

The other started and, to some extent dropping his mask, retorted:

"What are your conditions?"

"Rose Andrée, whom you have abducted and tormented, is dying in some hole or corner. Where is she?"

A strange thing occurred and impressed Rénine. Dalbrèque's face, usually so common, was lit up by a smile that made it almost attractive. But this was only a flashing vision: the man immediately resumed his hard and impassive expression.

"And suppose I refuse to speak?" he said.

"So much the worse for you. It means your arrest."

"I dare say; but it means the death of Rose Andrée. Who will release her?"

"You. You will speak now, or in an hour, or two hours hence at least. You will never have the heart to keep silent and let her die."

Dalbrèque shrugged his shoulders. Then, raising his hand, he said:

"I swear on my life that, if they arrest me, not a word will leave my lips."

"What then?"

"Then save me. We will meet this evening at the entrance to the Parc des Landes and say what we have to say."

"Why not at once?"

"I have spoken."

"Will you be there?"

"I shall be there."

Rénine reflected. There was something in all this that he failed to grasp. In any case, the frightful danger that threatened Rose Andrée dominated the whole situation; and Rénine was not the man to despise this threat and to persist out of vanity in a perilous course. Rose Andrée's life came before everything.

He struck several blows on the wall of the next bedroom and called his chauffeur.

"Adolphe, is the car ready?"

"Yes, sir."

"Set her going and pull her up in front of the terrace outside the café, right against the boxes so as to block the exit. As for you," he continued, addressing Dalbrèque, "you're to jump on your machine and, instead of making off along the road, cross the yard. At the end of the yard is a passage leading into a lane. There you will be free. But no hesitation and no blundering. . . else you'll get yourself nabbed. Good luck to you."

He waited till the car was drawn up in accordance with his instructions and, when he reached it, he began to question his chauffeur, in order to attract the detectives' attention.

One of them, however, having cast a glance through the spindle-trees, caught sight of Dalbrèque just as he reached the bottom of the staircase. He gave the alarm and darted forward, followed by his comrades, but had to run round the car and bumped into the chauffeur, which gave Dalbrèque time to mount his bicycle and cross the yard unimpeded. He thus had some seconds' start. Unfortunately for him as he was about to enter the passage at the back, a troop of boys and girls appeared, returning from vespers. On hearing the shouts of the detectives, they spread their arms in front of the fugitive, who gave two or three lurches and ended by falling.

Cries of triumph were raised:

"Lay hold of him! Stop him!" roared the detectives as they rushed forward.

Rénine, seeing that the game was up, ran after the others and called out:

"Stop him!"

He came up with them just as Dalbrèque, after regaining his feet, knocked one of the policemen down and levelled his revolver. Rénine snatched it out of his hands. But the two other detectives, startled, had also produced their weapons. They fired. Dalbrèque, hit in the leg and the chest, pitched forward and fell.

"Thank you, sir," said the inspector to Rénine introducing himself. "We owe a lot to you."

"It seems to me that you've done for the fellow," said Rénine. "Who is he?"

"One Dalbrèque, a scoundrel for whom we were looking."

Rénine was beside himself. Hortense had joined him by this time; and he growled:

"The silly fools! Now they've killed him!"

"Oh, it isn't possible!"

"We shall see. But, whether he's dead or alive, it's death to Rose Andrée. How are we to trace her? And what chance have we of finding the place—some inaccessible retreat—where the poor thing is dying of misery and starvation?"

The detectives and peasants had moved away, bearing Dalbrèque with them on an improvised stretcher. Rénine, who had at first followed them, in order to find out what was going to happen, changed his mind and was now standing with his eyes fixed on the ground. The fall of the bicycle had unfastened the parcel which Dalbrèque had tied to the handle-bar; and the newspaper had burst, revealing its contents, a tin saucepan, rusty, dented, battered and useless.

"What's the meaning of this?" he muttered. "What was the idea? . . ."

He picked it up examined it. Then he gave a grin and a click of the tongue and chuckled, slowly:

"Don't move an eyelash, my dear. Let all these people clear off. All this is no business of ours, is it? The troubles of police don't concern us. We are two motorists travelling for our pleasure and collecting old saucepans if we feel so inclined."

He called his chauffeur:

"Adolphe, take us to the Parc des Landes by a roundabout road."

Half an hour later they reached the sunken track and began to scramble down it on foot beside the wooded slopes. The Seine, which was very low at this time of day, was lapping against a little jetty near which lay a worm-eaten, mouldering boat, full of puddles of water.

Rénine stepped into the boat and at once began to bale out the puddles with his saucepan. He then drew the boat alongside of the jetty, helped Hortense in and used the one oar which he shipped in a gap in the stern to work her into midstream:

"I believe I'm there!" he said, with a laugh. "The worst that can happen to us is to get our feet wet, for our craft leaks a trifle. But haven't we a saucepan? Oh, blessings on that useful utensil! Almost as soon as I set eyes upon it, I remembered that people use those articles to bale out the bottoms of leaky boats. Why, there was bound to be a boat in the Landes woods! How was it I never thought of that? But of course Dalbrèque made use of her to cross the Seine! And, as she made water, he brought a saucepan."

"Then Rose Andrée. . . ?" asked Hortense.

"Is a prisoner on the other bank, on the Jumièges peninsula. You see the famous abbey from here."

They ran aground on a beach of big pebbles covered with slime.

"And it can't be very far away," he added. "Dalbrèque did not spend the whole night running about."

A tow-path followed the deserted bank. Another path led away from it. They chose the second and, passing between orchards enclosed by hedges, came to a landscape that seemed strangely familiar to them. Where had they seen that pool before, with the willows overhanging it? And where had they seen that abandoned hovel?

Suddenly both of them stopped with one accord:

"Oh!" said Hortense. "I can hardly believe my eyes!"

Opposite them was the white gate of a large orchard, at the back of which, among groups of old, gnarled apple-trees, appeared a cottage with blue shutters, the cottage of the Happy Princess.

"Of course!" cried Rénine. "And I ought to have known it, considering that the film showed both this cottage and the forest close by. And isn't everything happening exactly as in *The Happy Princess*? Isn't Dalbrèque dominated by the memory of it? The house, which is certainly the one in which Rose Andrée spent the summer, was empty. He has shut her up there."

"But the house, you told me, was in the Seine-inférieure."

"Well, so are we! To the left of the river, the Eure and the forest of Brotonne; to the right, the Seine-inférieure. But between them is the obstacle of the river, which is why I didn't connect the two. A hundred and fifty yards of water form a more effective division than dozens of miles."

The gate was locked. They got through the hedge a little lower down and walked towards the house, which was screened on one side by an old wall shaggy with ivy and roofed with thatch.

"It seems as if there was somebody there," said Hortense. "Didn't I hear the sound of a window?"

"Listen."

Some one struck a few chords on a piano. Then a voice arose, a woman's voice softly and solemnly singing a ballad that thrilled with restrained passion. The woman's whole soul seemed to breathe itself into the melodious notes.

They walked on. The wall concealed them from view, but they saw a sitting-room furnished with bright wall-paper and a blue Roman carpet. The throbbing voice ceased. The piano ended with a last chord; and the singer rose and appeared framed in the window.

"Rose Andrée!" whispered Hortense.

"Well!" said Rénine, admitting his astonishment. "This is the last thing that I expected! Rose Andrée! Rose Andrée at liberty! And singing Massenet in the sitting room of her cottage!"

"What does it all mean? Do you understand?"

"Yes, but it has taken me long enough! But how could we have guessed. . . ?"

Although they had never seen her except on the screen, they had not the least doubt that this was she. It was really Rose Andrée, or rather, the Happy Princess, whom they had admired a few days before, amidst the furniture of that very sitting-room or on the threshold of that very cottage. She was wearing the same dress; her hair was done in the same way; she had on the same bangles and necklaces as in *The Happy Princess*; and her lovely face, with its rosy cheeks and laughing eyes, bore the same look of joy and serenity.

Some sound must have caught her ear, for she leant over towards a clump of shrubs beside the cottage and whispered into the silent garden:

"Georges. . . Georges. . . Is that you, my darling?"

Receiving no reply, she drew herself up and stood smiling at the happy thoughts that seemed to flood her being.

But a door opened at the back of the room and an old peasant woman entered with a tray laden with bread, butter and milk:

"Here, Rose, my pretty one, I've brought you your supper. Milk fresh from the cow. . ."

And, putting down the tray, she continued:

"Aren't you afraid, Rose, of the chill of the night air? Perhaps you're expecting your sweetheart?"

"I haven't a sweetheart, my dear old Catherine."

"What next!" said the old woman, laughing. "Only this morning there were footprints under the window that didn't look at all proper!"

"A burglar's footprints perhaps, Catherine."

"Well, I don't say they weren't, Rose dear, especially as in your calling you have a lot of people round you whom it's well to be careful of. For instance, your friend Dalbrèque, eh? Nice goings on his are! You saw the paper yesterday. A fellow who has robbed and murdered people and carried off a woman at Le Havre. . . !"

Hortense and Rénine would have much liked to know what Rose Andrée thought of the revelations, but she had turned her back to them and was sitting at her supper; and the window was now closed, so that they could neither hear her reply nor see the expression of her features.

They waited for a moment. Hortense was listening with an anxious face. But Rénine began to laugh:

"Very funny, really funny! And such an unexpected ending! And we who were hunting for her in some cave or damp cellar, a horrible tomb where the poor thing was dying of hunger! It's a fact, she knew the terrors of that first night of captivity; and I maintain that, on that first night, she was flung, half-dead, into the cave. Only, there you are: the next morning she was alive! One night was enough to tame the little rogue and to make Dalbrèque as handsome as Prince Charming in her eyes! For see the difference. On the films or in novels, the Happy Princesses resist or commit suicide. But in real life. . . oh, woman, woman!"

"Yes," said Hortense, "but the man she loves is almost certainly dead."

"And a good thing too! It would be the best solution. What would be the outcome of this criminal love for a thief and murderer?"

A few minutes passed. Then, amid the peaceful silence of the waning day, mingled with the first shadows of the twilight, they again heard the grating of the window, which was cautiously opened. Rose Andrée leant over the garden and waited, with her eyes turned to the wall, as though she saw something there.

Presently, Rénine shook the ivy-branches.

"Ah!" she said. "This time I know you're there! Yes, the ivy's moving. Georges, Georges darling, why do you keep me waiting? Catherine has gone. I am all alone. . ."

She had knelt down and was distractedly stretching out her shapely arms covered with bangles which clashed with a metallic sound:

"Georges! . . . Georges! . . ."

Her every movement, the thrill of her voice, her whole being expressed desire and love. Hortense, deeply touched, could not help saying:

"How the poor thing loves him! If she but knew. . ."

"Ah!" cried the girl. "You've spoken. You're there, and you want me to come to you, don't you? Here I am, Georges! . . ."

She climbed over the window-ledge and began to run, while Rénine went round the wall and advanced to meet her.

She stopped short in front of him and stood choking at the sight of this man and woman whom she did not know and who were stepping out of the very shadow from which her beloved appeared to her each night.

Rénine bowed, gave his name and introduced his companion:

"Madame Hortense Daniel, a pupil and friend of your mother's."

Still motionless with stupefaction, her features drawn, she stammered:

"You know who I am? . . . And you were there just now? . . . You heard what I was saying. . . ?"

Rénine, without hesitating or pausing in his speech, said:

"You are Rose Andrée, the Happy Princess. We saw you on the films the other evening; and circumstances led us to set out in search of you. . . to Le Havre, where you were abducted on the day when you were to have left for America, and to the forest of Brotonne, where you were imprisoned."

She protested eagerly, with a forced laugh:

"What is all this? I have not been to Le Havre. I came straight here. Abducted? Imprisoned? What nonsense!"

"Yes, imprisoned, in the same cave as the Happy Princess; and you broke off some branches to the right of the cave."

"But how absurd! Who would have abducted me? I have no enemy."

"There is a man in love with you: the one whom you were expecting just now."

"Yes, my lover," she said, proudly. "Have I not the right to receive whom I like?"

"You have the right; you are a free agent. But the man who comes to see you every evening is wanted by the police. His name is Georges Dalbrèque. He killed Bourguet the jeweller."

The accusation made her start with indignation and she exclaimed:

"It's a lie! An infamous fabrication of the newspapers! Georges was in Paris on the night of the murder. He can prove it."

"He stole a motor car and forty thousand francs in notes."

She retorted vehemently:

"The motor-car was taken back by his friends and the notes will be restored. He never touched them. My leaving for America had made him lose his head."

"Very well. I am quite willing to believe everything that you say. But the police may show less faith in these statements and less indulgence."

She became suddenly uneasy and faltered:

"The police. . . There's nothing to fear from them. . . They won't know. . ."

"Where to find him? I succeeded, at all events. He's working as a woodcutter, in the forest of Brotonne."

"Yes, but. . . you. . . that was an accident. . . whereas the police. . ."

The words left her lips with the greatest difficulty. Her voice was trembling. And suddenly she rushed at Rénine, stammering:

"He is arrested? . . . I am sure of it! . . . And you have come to tell me. . . Arrested! Wounded! Dead perhaps? . . . Oh, please, please! . . ."

She had no strength left. All her pride, all the certainty of her great love gave way to an immense despair and she sobbed out.

"No, he's not dead, is he? No, I feel that he's not dead. Oh, sir, how unjust it all is! He's the gentlest man, the best that ever lived. He has changed my whole life. Everything is different since I began to love him. And I love him so! I love him! I want to go to him. Take me to him. I want them to arrest me too. I love him. . . I could not live without him. . ."

An impulse of sympathy made Hortense put her arms around the girl's neck and say warmly:

"Yes, come. He is not dead, I am sure, only wounded; and Prince Rénine will save him. You will, won't you, Rénine? . . . Come. Make up a story for your servant: say that you're going somewhere by train and that she is not to tell anybody. Be quick. Put on a wrap. We will save him, I swear we will."

Rose Andrée went indoors and returned almost at once, disguised beyond recognition in a long cloak and a veil that shrouded her face; and they all took the road back to Routot. At the inn, Rose Andrée passed as a friend whom they had been to fetch in the neighbourhood and were taking to Paris with them. Rénine ran out to make enquiries and came back to the two women.

"It's all right. Dalbrèque is alive. They have put him to bed in a private room at the mayor's offices. He has a broken leg and a rather high temperature; but all the same they expect to move him to Rouen to-morrow and they have telephoned there for a motor-car."

"And then?" asked Rose Andrée, anxiously.

Rénine smiled:

"Why, then we shall leave at daybreak. We shall take up our positions in a sunken road, rifle in hand, attack the motor-coach and carry off Georges!"

"Oh, don't laugh!" she said, plaintively. "I am so unhappy!"

But the adventure seemed to amuse Rénine; and, when he was alone with Hortense, he exclaimed:

"You see what comes of preferring dishonour to death! But hang it all, who could have expected this? It isn't a bit the way in which things happen in the pictures! Once the man of the woods had carried off his victim and considering that for three weeks there was no one to defend her, how could we imagine—we who had been proceeding all along under the influence of the pictures—that in the space of a few hours the victim would become a princess in love? Confound that Georges! I now understand the sly, humorous look which I surprised on his mobile features! He remembered, Georges did, and he didn't care a hang for me! Oh, he tricked me nicely! And you, my dear, he tricked you too! And it was all the influence of the film. They show us, at the cinema, a brute beast, a sort of long-haired, ape-faced savage. What can a man like that be in real life? A brute, inevitably, don't you agree? Well, he's nothing of the kind; he's a Don Juan! The humbug!"

"You will save him, won't you?" said Hortense, in a beseeching tone.

"Are you very anxious that I should?"

"Very."

"In that case, promise to give me your hand to kiss."

"You can have both hands, Rénine, and gladly."

The night was uneventful. Rénine had given orders for the two ladies to be waked at an early hour. When they came down, the motor was leaving the yard and pulling up in front of the inn. It was raining; and Adolphe, the chauffeur, had fixed up the long, low hood and packed the luggage inside.

Rénine called for his bill. They all three took a cup of coffee. But, just as they were leaving the room, one of the inspector's men came rushing in:

"Have you seen him?" he asked. "Isn't he here?"

The inspector himself arrived at a run, greatly excited:

"The prisoner has escaped! He ran back through the inn! He can't be far away!"

A dozen rustics appeared like a whirlwind. They ransacked the lofts, the stables, the sheds. They scattered over the neighbourhood. But the search led to no discovery.

"Oh, hang it all!" said Rénine, who had taken his part in the hunt. "How can it have happened?"

"How do I know?" spluttered the inspector in despair. "I left my three men watching in the next room. I found them this morning fast asleep, stupefied by some narcotic which had been mixed with their wine! And the Dalbrèque bird had flown!"

"Which way?"

"Through the window. There were evidently accomplices, with ropes and a ladder. And, as Dalbrèque had a broken leg, they carried him off on the stretcher itself."

"They left no traces?"

"No traces of footsteps, true. The rain has messed everything up. But they went through the yard, because the stretcher's there."

"You'll find him, Mr. Inspector, there's no doubt of that. In any case, you may be sure that you won't have any trouble over the affair. I shall be in Paris this evening and shall go straight to the prefecture, where I have influential friends."

Rénine went back to the two women in the coffee-room and Hortense at once said:

"It was you who carried him off, wasn't it? Please put Rose Andrée's mind at rest. She is so terrified!"

He gave Rose Andrée his arm and led her to the car. She was staggering and very pale; and she said, in a faint voice:

"Are we going? And he: is he safe? Won't they catch him again?"

Looking deep into her eyes, he said:

"Swear to me, Rose Andrée, that in two months, when he is well and when I have proved his innocence, swear that you will go away with him to America."

"I swear."

"And that, once there, you will marry him."

"I swear."

He spoke a few words in her ear.

"Ah!" she said. "May Heaven bless you for it!"

Hortense took her seat in front, with Rénine, who sat at the wheel. The inspector, hat in hand, fussed around the car until it moved off.

They drove through the forest, crossed the Seine at La Mailleraie and struck into the Havre-Rouen road.

"Take off your glove and give me your hand to kiss," Rénine ordered. "You promised that you would."

"Oh!" said Hortense. "But it was to be when Dalbrèque was saved."

"He is saved."

"Not yet. The police are after him. They may catch him again. He will not be really saved until he is with Rose Andrée."

"He is with Rose Andrée," he declared.

"What do you mean?"

"Turn round."

She did so.

In the shadow of the hood, right at the back, behind the chauffeur, Rose Andrée was kneeling beside a man lying on the seat.

"Oh," stammered Hortense, "it's incredible! Then it was you who hid him last night? And he was there, in front of the inn, when the inspector was seeing us off?"

"Lord, yes! He was there, under the cushions and rugs!"

"It's incredible!" she repeated, utterly bewildered. "It's incredible! How were you able to manage it all?"

"I wanted to kiss your hand," he said.

She removed her glove, as he bade her, and raised her hand to his lips.

The car was speeding between the peaceful Seine and the white cliffs that border it. They sat silent for a long while. Then he said:

"I had a talk with Dalbrèque last night. He's a fine fellow and is ready to do anything for Rose Andrée. He's right. A man must do anything for the woman he loves. He must devote himself to her, offer her all that is beautiful in this world: joy and happiness. . . and, if she should be bored, stirring adventures to distract her, to excite her and to make her smile. . . or even weep."

Hortense shivered; and her eyes were not quite free from tears. For the first time he was alluding to the sentimental adventure that bound them by a tie which as yet was frail, but which became stronger and more enduring with each of the ventures on which they entered together, pursuing them feverishly and anxiously to their close. Already she felt powerless and uneasy with this extraordinary man, who subjected events to his will and seemed to play with the destinies of those whom he fought or protected. He filled her with dread and at the same time he attracted her. She thought of him sometimes as her master, sometimes as an enemy against whom she must defend herself, but oftenest as a perturbing friend, full of charm and fascination. . .

V

Thérèse and Germaine

The weather was so mild that autumn that, on the 12th of October, in the morning, several families still lingering in their villas at Étretat had gone down to the beach. The sea, lying between the cliffs and the clouds on the horizon, might have suggested a mountain-lake slumbering in the hollow of the enclosing rocks, were it not for that crispness in the air and those pale, soft and indefinite colours in the sky which give a special charm to certain days in Normandy.

"It's delicious," murmured Hortense. But the next moment she added: "All the same, we did not come here to enjoy the spectacle of nature or to wonder whether that huge stone Needle on our left was really at one time the home of Arsène Lupin."

"We came here," said Prince Rénine, "because of the conversation which I overheard, a fortnight ago, in a dining-car, between a man and a woman."

"A conversation of which I was unable to catch a single word."

"If those two people could have guessed for an instant that it was possible to hear a single word of what they were saying, they would not have spoken, for their conversation was one of extraordinary gravity and importance. But I have very sharp ears; and though I could not follow every sentence, I insist that we may be certain of two things. First, that man and woman, who are brother and sister, have an appointment at a quarter to twelve this morning, the 12th of October, at the spot known as the Trois Mathildes, with a third person, who is married and who wishes at all costs to recover his or her liberty. Secondly, this appointment, at which they will come to a final agreement, is to be followed this evening by a walk along the cliffs, when the third person will bring with him or her the man or woman, I can't definitely say which, whom they want to get rid of. That is the gist of the whole thing. Now, as I know a spot called the Trois Mathildes some way above Étretat and as this is not an everyday name, we came down yesterday to thwart the plan of these objectionable persons."

"What plan?" asked Hortense. "For, after all, it's only your assumption that there's to be a victim and that the victim is to be flung off the top of the cliffs. You yourself told me that you heard no allusion to a possible murder."

"That is so. But I heard some very plain words relating to the marriage of the brother or the sister with the wife or the husband of the third person, which implies the need for a crime."

They were sitting on the terrace of the casino, facing the stairs which run down to the beach. They therefore overlooked the few privately-owned cabins on the shingle, where a party of four men were playing bridge, while a group of ladies sat talking and knitting.

A short distance away and nearer to the sea was another cabin, standing by itself and closed.

Half-a-dozen bare-legged children were paddling in the water.

"No," said Hortense, "all this autumnal sweetness and charm fails to attract me. I have so much faith in all your theories that I can't help thinking, in spite of everything, of this dreadful problem. Which of those people yonder is threatened? Death has already selected its victim. Who is it? Is it that young, fair-haired woman, rocking herself and laughing? Is it that tall man over there, smoking his cigar? And which of them has the thought of murder hidden in his heart? All the people we see are quietly enjoying themselves. Yet death is prowling among them."

"Capital!" said Rénine. "You too are becoming enthusiastic. What did I tell you? The whole of life's an adventure; and nothing but adventure is worth while. At the first breath of coming events, there you are, quivering in every nerve. You share in all the tragedies stirring around you; and the feeling of mystery awakens in the depths of your being. See, how closely you are observing that couple who have just arrived. You never can tell: that may be the gentleman who proposes to do away with his wife? Or perhaps the lady contemplates making away with her husband?"

"The d'Ormevals? Never! A perfectly happy couple! Yesterday, at the hotel, I had a long talk with the wife. And you yourself. . ."

"Oh, I played a round of golf with Jacques d'Ormeval, who rather fancies himself as an athlete, and I played at dolls with their two charming little girls!"

The d'Ormevals came up and exchanged a few words with them. Madame d'Ormeval said that her two daughters had gone back to Paris that morning with their governess. Her husband, a great tall fellow with a yellow beard, carrying his blazer over his arm and puffing out his chest under a cellular shirt, complained of the heat:

"Have you the key of the cabin, Thérèse?" he asked his wife, when they had left Rénine and Hortense and stopped at the top of the stairs, a few yards away.

"Here it is," said the wife. "Are you going to read your papers?"

"Yes. Unless we go for a stroll? . . ."

"I had rather wait till the afternoon: do you mind? I have a lot of letters to write this morning."

"Very well. We'll go on the cliff."

Hortense and Rénine exchanged a glance of surprise. Was this suggestion accidental? Or had they before them, contrary to their expectations, the very couple of whom they were in search?

Hortense tried to laugh:

"My heart is thumping," she said. "Nevertheless, I absolutely refuse to believe in anything so improbable. 'My husband and I have never had the slightest quarrel,' she said to me. No, it's quite clear that those two get on admirably."

"We shall see presently, at the Trois Mathildes, if one of them comes to meet the brother and sister."

M. d'Ormeval had gone down the stairs, while his wife stood leaning on the balustrade of the terrace. She had a beautiful, slender, supple figure. Her clear-cut profile was emphasized by a rather too prominent chin when at rest; and, when it was not smiling, the face gave an expression of sadness and suffering.

"Have you lost something, Jacques?" she called out to her husband, who was stooping over the shingle.

"Yes, the key," he said. "It slipped out of my hand."

She went down to him and began to look also. For two or three minutes, as they sheered off to the right and remained close to the bottom of the under-cliff, they were invisible to Hortense and Rénine. Their voices were covered by the noise of a dispute which had arisen among the bridge-players.

They reappeared almost simultaneously. Madame d'Ormeval slowly climbed a few steps of the stairs and then stopped and turned her face towards the sea. Her husband had thrown his blazer over his shoulders and was making for the isolated cabin. As he passed the bridge-players, they asked him for a decision, pointing to their cards spread out upon the table. But, with a wave of the hand, he refused to give an opinion and walked on, covered the thirty yards which divided them from the cabin, opened the door and went in.

Thérèse d'Ormeval came back to the terrace and remained for ten minutes sitting on a bench. Then she came out through the casino. Hortense, on leaning forward, saw her entering one of the chalets annexed to the Hôtel Hauville and, a moment later, caught sight of her again on the balcony.

"Eleven o'clock," said Rénine. "Whoever it is, he or she, or one of the card-players, or one of their wives, it won't be long before some one goes to the appointed place."

Nevertheless, twenty minutes passed and twenty-five; and no one stirred.

"Perhaps Madame d'Ormeval has gone." Hortense suggested, anxiously. "She is no longer on her balcony."

"If she is at the Trois Mathildes," said Rénine, "we will go and catch her there."

He was rising to his feet, when a fresh discussion broke out among the bridge-players and one of them exclaimed:

"Let's put it to d'Ormeval."

"Very well," said his adversary. "I'll accept his decision. . . if he consents to act as umpire. He was rather huffy just now."

They called out:

"D'Ormeval! D'Ormeval!"

They then saw that d'Ormeval must have shut the door behind him, which kept him in the half dark, the cabin being one of the sort that has no window.

"He's asleep," cried one. "Let's wake him up."

All four went to the cabin, began by calling to him and, on receiving no answer, thumped on the door:

"Hi! D'Ormeval! Are you asleep?"

On the terrace Serge Rénine suddenly leapt to his feet with so uneasy an air that Hortense was astonished. He muttered:

"If only it's not too late!"

And, when Hortense asked him what he meant, he tore down the steps and started running to the cabin. He reached it just as the bridge-players were trying to break in the door:

"Stop!" he ordered. "Things must be done in the regular fashion."

"What things?" they asked.

He examined the Venetian shutters at the top of each of the folding-doors and, on finding that one of the upper slats was partly broken, hung on as best he could to the roof of the cabin and cast a glance inside. Then he said to the four men:

"I was right in thinking that, if M. d'Ormeval did not reply, he must have been prevented by some serious cause. There is every reason to believe that M. d'Ormeval is wounded. . . or dead."

"Dead!" they cried. "What do you mean? He has only just left us."

Rénine took out his knife, prized open the lock and pulled back the two doors.

There were shouts of dismay. M. d'Ormeval was lying flat on his face, clutching his jacket and his newspaper in his hands. Blood was flowing from his back and staining his shirt.

"Oh!" said some one. "He has killed himself!"

"How can he have killed himself?" said Rénine. "The wound is right in the middle of the back, at a place which the hand can't reach. And, besides, there's not a knife in the cabin."

The others protested:

"If so, he has been murdered. But that's impossible! There has been nobody here. We should have seen, if there had been. Nobody could have passed us without our seeing. . ."

The other men, all the ladies and the children paddling in the sea had come running up. Rénine allowed no one to enter the cabin, except a doctor who was present. But the doctor could only say that M. d'Ormeval was dead, stabbed with a dagger.

At that moment, the mayor and the policeman arrived, together with some people of the village. After the usual enquiries, they carried away the body.

A few persons went on ahead to break the news to Thérèse d'Ormeval, who was once more to be seen on her balcony.

AND SO THE TRAGEDY HAD taken place without any clue to explain how a man, protected by a closed door with an uninjured lock, could have been murdered in the space of a few minutes and in front of twenty witnesses, one might almost say, twenty spectators. No one had entered the cabin. No one had come out of it. As for the dagger with which M. d'Ormeval had been stabbed between the shoulders, it could not be traced. And all this would have suggested the idea of a trick of sleight-of-hand performed by a clever conjuror, had it not concerned a terrible murder, committed under the most mysterious conditions.

Hortense was unable to follow, as Rénine would have liked, the small party who were making for Madame d'Ormeval; she was paralysed with excitement and incapable of moving. It was the first time that her adventures with Rénine had taken her into the very heart of the action and that, instead of noting the consequences of a murder, or assisting in the pursuit of the criminals, she found herself confronted with the murder itself.

It left her trembling all over; and she stammered: "How horrible! . . . The poor fellow! . . . Ah, Rénine, you couldn't save him this time! . . . And that's what upsets me more than anything, that we could and should have saved him, since we knew of the plot. . ."

Rénine made her sniff at a bottle of salts; and when she had quite recovered her composure, he said, while observing her attentively:

"So you think that there is some connection between the murder and the plot which we were trying to frustrate?"

"Certainly," said she, astonished at the question.

"Then, as that plot was hatched by a husband against his wife or by a wife against her husband, you admit that Madame d'Ormeval. . . ?"

"Oh, no, impossible!" she said. "To begin with, Madame d'Ormeval did not leave her rooms. . . and then I shall never believe that pretty woman capable. . . No, no, of course there was something else. . ."

"What else?"

"I don't know. . . You may have misunderstood what the brother and sister were saying to each other. . . You see, the murder has been committed under quite different conditions. . . at another hour and another place. . ."

"And therefore," concluded Rénine, "the two cases are not in any way related?"

"Oh," she said, "there's no making it out! It's all so strange!"

Rénine became a little satirical:

"My pupil is doing me no credit to-day," he said. "Why, here is a perfectly simple story, unfolded before your eyes. You have seen it reeled off like a scene in the cinema; and it all remains as obscure to you as though you were hearing of an affair that happened in a cave a hundred miles away!"

Hortense was confounded:

"What are you saying? Do you mean that you have understood it? What clues have you to go by?"

Rénine looked at his watch:

"I have not understood everything," he said. "The murder itself, the mere brutal murder, yes. But the essential thing, that is to say, the psychology of the crime: I've no clue to that. Only, it is twelve o'clock. The brother and sister, seeing no one come to the appointment at the Trois Mathildes, will go down to the beach. Don't you think that we shall learn something then of the accomplice whom I accuse them of having and of the connection between the two cases?"

They reached the esplanade in front of the Hauville chalets, with the capstans by which the fishermen haul up their boats to the beach. A number of inquisitive persons were standing outside the door of one of the chalets. Two coastguards, posted at the door, prevented them from entering.

The mayor shouldered his way eagerly through the crowd. He was back from the post-office, where he had been telephoning to Le Havre, to the office of the procurator-general, and had been told that the public prosecutor and an examining-magistrate would come on to Étretat in the course of the afternoon.

"That leaves us plenty of time for lunch," said Rénine. "The tragedy will not be enacted before two or three o'clock. And I have an idea that it will be sensational."

They hurried nevertheless. Hortense, overwrought by fatigue and her desire to know what was happening, continually questioned Rénine, who replied evasively, with his eyes turned to the esplanade, which they could see through the windows of the coffee-room.

"Are you watching for those two?" asked Hortense.

"Yes, the brother and sister."

"Are you sure that they will venture? . . ."

"Look out! Here they come!"

He went out quickly.

Where the main street opened on the sea-front, a lady and gentleman were advancing with hesitating steps, as though unfamiliar with the place. The brother was a puny little man, with a sallow complexion. He was wearing a motoring-cap. The sister too was short, but rather stout, and was wrapped in a large cloak. She struck them as a woman of a certain age, but still good-looking under the thin veil that covered her face.

They saw the groups of bystanders and drew nearer. Their gait betrayed uneasiness and hesitation.

The sister asked a question of a seaman. At the first words of his answer, which no doubt conveyed the news of d'Ormeval's death, she uttered a cry and tried to force her way through the crowd. The brother, learning in his turn what had happened, made great play with his elbows and shouted to the coast-guards:

"I'm a friend of d'Ormeval's! . . . Here's my card! Frédéric Astaing. . . My sister, Germaine Astaing, knows Madame d'Ormeval intimately! . . . They were expecting us. . . We had an appointment! . . ."

They were allowed to pass. Rénine, who had slipped behind them, followed them in without a word, accompanied by Hortense.

The d'Ormevals had four bedrooms and a sitting-room on the second floor. The sister rushed into one of the rooms and threw herself on her knees beside the bed on which the corpse lay stretched. Thérèse d'Ormeval was in the sitting-room and was sobbing in the midst of a small company of silent persons. The brother sat down beside her, eagerly seized her hands and said, in a trembling voice:

"My poor friend! . . . My poor friend! . . ."

Rénine and Hortense gazed at the pair of them: and Hortense whispered:

"And she's supposed to have killed him for that? Impossible!"

"Nevertheless," observed Rénine, "they are acquaintances; and we know that Astaing and his sister were also acquainted with a third person who was their accomplice. So that. . ."

"It's impossible!" Hortense repeated.

And, in spite of all presumption, she felt so much attracted by Thérèse that, when Frédéric Astaing stood up, she proceeded straightway to sit down beside her and consoled her in a gentle voice. The unhappy woman's tears distressed her profoundly.

Rénine, on the other hand, applied himself from the outset to watching the brother and sister, as though this were the only thing that mattered, and did not take his eyes off Frédéric Astaing, who, with an air of indifference, began to make a minute inspection of the premises, examining the sitting-room, going into all the bedrooms, mingling with the various groups of persons present and asking questions about the manner in which the murder had been committed. Twice his sister came up and spoke to him. Then he went back to Madame d'Ormeval and again sat down beside her, full of earnest sympathy. Lastly, in the lobby, he had a long conversation with his sister, after which they parted, like people who have come to a perfect understanding. Frédéric then left. These manoeuvers had lasted quite thirty or forty minutes.

It was at this moment that the motor-car containing the examining-magistrate and the public prosecutor pulled up outside the chalets. Rénine, who did not expect them until later, said to Hortense:

"We must be quick. On no account leave Madame d'Ormeval."

Word was sent up to the persons whose evidence might be of any service that they were to go to the beach, where the magistrate was beginning a preliminary investigation. He would call on Madame d'Ormeval afterwards. Accordingly, all who were present left the chalet. No one remained behind except the two guards and Germaine Astaing.

Germaine knelt down for the last time beside the dead man and, bending low, with her face in her hands, prayed for a long time. Then she rose and was opening the door on the landing, when Rénine came forward:

"I should like a few words with you, madame."

She seemed surprised and replied:

"What is it, monsieur? I am listening."

"Not here."

"Where then, monsieur?"

"Next door, in the sitting-room."

"No," she said, sharply.

"Why not? Though you did not even shake hands with her, I presume that Madame d'Ormeval is your friend?"

He gave her no time to reflect, drew her into the next room, closed the door and, at once pouncing upon Madame d'Ormeval, who was trying to go out and return to her own room, said:

"No, madame, listen, I implore you. Madame Astaing's presence need not drive you away. We have very serious matters to discuss, without losing a minute."

The two women, standing face to face, were looking at each other with the same expression of implacable hatred, in which might be read the same confusion of spirit and the same restrained anger. Hortense, who believed them to be friends and who might, up to a certain point, have believed them to be accomplices, foresaw with terror the hostile encounter which she felt to be inevitable. She compelled Madame d'Ormeval to resume her seat, while Rénine took up his position in the middle of the room and spoke in resolute tones:

"Chance, which has placed me in possession of part of the truth, will enable me to save you both, if you are willing to assist me with a frank explanation that will give me the particulars which I still need. Each of you knows the danger in which she stands, because each of you is conscious in her heart of the evil for which she is responsible. But you are carried away by hatred; and it is for me to see clearly and to act. The examining-magistrate will be here in half-an-hour. By that time, you must have come to an agreement."

They both started, as though offended by such a word.

"Yes, an agreement," he repeated, in a more imperious tone. "Whether you like it or not, you will come to an agreement. You are not the only ones to be considered. There are your two little daughters, Madame d'Ormeval. Since circumstances have set me in their path, I am intervening in their defence and for their safety. A blunder, a word too much; and they are ruined. That must not happen."

At the mention of her children, Madame d'Ormeval broke down and sobbed. Germaine Astaing shrugged her shoulders and made a movement towards the door. Rénine once more blocked the way:

"Where are you going?"

"I have been summoned by the examining-magistrate."

"No, you have not."

"Yes, I have. Just as all those have been who have any evidence to give."

"You were not on the spot. You know nothing of what happened. Nobody knows anything of the murder."

"I know who committed it."

"That's impossible."

"It was Thérèse d'Ormeval."

The accusation was hurled forth in an outburst of rage and with a fiercely threatening gesture.

"You wretched creature!" exclaimed madame d'Ormeval, rushing at her. "Go! Leave the room! Oh, what a wretch the woman is!"

Hortense was trying to restrain her, but Rénine whispered:

"Let them be. It's what I wanted. . . to pitch them one against the other and so to let in the day-light."

Madame Astaing had made a convulsive effort to ward off the insult with a jest; and she sniggered:

"A wretched creature? Why? Because I have accused you?"

"Why? For every reason! You're a wretched creature! You hear what I say, Germaine: you're a wretch!"

Thérèse d'Ormeval was repeating the insult as though it afforded her some relief. Her anger was abating. Very likely also she no longer had the strength to keep up the struggle; and it was Madame Astaing who returned to the attack, with her fists clenched and her face distorted and suddenly aged by fully twenty years:

"You! You dare to insult me, you! You after the murder you have committed! You dare to lift up your head when the man whom you killed is lying in there on his death-bed! Ah, if one of us is a wretched creature, it's you, Thérèse, and you know it! You have killed your husband! You have killed your husband!"

She leapt forward, in the excitement of the terrible words which she was uttering; and her finger-nails were almost touching her friend's face.

"Oh, don't tell me you didn't kill him!" she cried. "Don't say that: I won't let you. Don't say it. The dagger is there, in your bag. My brother felt it, while he was talking to you; and his hand came out with stains of blood upon it: your husband's blood, Thérèse. And then, even if I had not discovered anything, do you think that I should not have guessed, in the first few minutes? Why, I knew the truth at once, Thérèse! When a sailor down there answered, 'M. d'Ormeval? He has been murdered,' I said to myself then and there, 'It's she, it's Thérèse, she killed him.'"

Thérèse did not reply. She had abandoned her attitude of protest. Hortense, who was watching her with anguish, thought that she could perceive in her the despondency of those who know themselves to be lost. Her cheeks had fallen in and she wore such an expression of despair that Hortense, moved to compassion, implored her to defend herself:

"Please, please, explain things. When the murder was committed, you were here, on the balcony. . . But then the dagger. . . how did you come to have it. . . ? How do you explain it? . . ."

"Explanations!" sneered Germaine Astaing. "How could she possibly explain? What do outward appearances matter? What does it matter what any one saw or did not see? The proof is the thing that tells. . . The dagger is there, in your bag, Thérèse: that's a fact. . . Yes, yes, it was you who did it! You killed him! You killed him in the end! . . . Ah, how often I've told my brother, 'She will kill him yet!' Frédéric used to try to defend you. He always had a weakness for you. But in his innermost heart he foresaw what would happen. . . And now the horrible thing has been done. A stab in the back! Coward! Coward! . . . And you would have me say nothing? Why, I didn't hesitate a moment! Nor did Frédéric. We looked for proofs at once. . . And I've denounced you of my own free will, perfectly well aware of what I was doing. . . And it's over, Thérèse. You're done for. Nothing can save you now. The dagger is in that bag which you are clutching in your hand. The magistrate is coming; and the dagger will be found, stained with the blood of your husband. So will your pocket-book. They're both there. And they will be found. . ."

Her rage had incensed her so vehemently that she was unable to continue and stood with her hand outstretched and her chin twitching with nervous tremors.

Rénine gently took hold of Madame d'Ormeval's bag. She clung to it, but he insisted and said:

"Please allow me, madame. Your friend Germaine is right. The examining-magistrate will be here presently; and the fact that the dagger and the pocket-book are in your possession will lead to your immediate arrest. This must not happen. Please allow me."

His insinuating voice diminished Thérèse d'Ormeval's resistance. She released her fingers, one by one. He took the bag, opened it, produced a little dagger with an ebony handle and a grey leather pocket-book and quietly slipped the two into the inside pocket of his jacket.

Germaine Astaing gazed at him in amazement: "You're mad, monsieur! What right have you. . . ?"

"These things must not be left lying about. I sha'n't worry now. The magistrate will never look for them in my pocket."

"But I shall denounce you to the police," she exclaimed, indignantly. "They shall be told!"

"No, no," he said, laughing, "you won't say anything! The police have nothing to do with this. The quarrel between you must be settled in private. What an idea, to go dragging the police into every incident of one's life!"

Madame Astaing was choking with fury:

"But you have no right to talk like this, monsieur! Who are you, after all? A friend of that woman's?"

"Since you have been attacking her, yes."

"But I'm only attacking her because she's guilty. For you can't deny it: she has killed her husband."

"I don't deny it," said Rénine, calmly. "We are all agreed on that point. Jacques d'Ormeval was killed by his wife. But, I repeat, the police must not know the truth."

"They shall know it through me, monsieur, I swear they shall. That woman must be punished: she has committed murder."

Rénine went up to her and, touching her on the shoulder:

"You asked me just now by what right I was interfering. And you yourself, madame?"

"I was a friend of Jacques d'Ormeval."

"Only a friend?"

She was a little taken aback, but at once pulled herself together and replied:

"I was his friend and it is my duty to avenge his death."

"Nevertheless, you will remain silent, as he did."

"He did not know, when he died."

"That's where you are wrong. He could have accused his wife, if he had wished. He had ample time to accuse her; and he said nothing."

"Why?"

"Because of his children."

Madame Astaing was not appeased; and her attitude displayed the same longing for revenge and the same detestation. But she was influenced by Rénine in spite of herself. In the small, closed room, where there was such a clash of hatred, he was gradually becoming the master; and Germaine Astaing understood that it was against him that she had to struggle, while Madame d'Ormeval felt all the comfort of that unexpected support which was offering itself on the brink of the abyss:

"Thank you, monsieur," she said. "As you have seen all this so clearly, you also know that it was for my children's sake that I did not give myself up. But for that. . . I am so tired. . . !"

And so the scene was changing and things assuming a different aspect. Thanks to a few words let fall in the midst of the dispute, the culprit was lifting her head and taking heart, whereas her accuser was hesitating and seemed to be uneasy. And it also came about that the accuser dared not say anything further and that the culprit was nearing the moment at which the need is felt of breaking silence and of speaking, quite naturally, words that are at once a confession and a relief.

"The time, I think, has come," said Rénine to Thérèse, with the same unvarying gentleness, "when you can and ought to explain yourself."

She was again weeping, lying huddled in a chair. She too revealed a face aged and ravaged by sorrow; and, in a very low voice, with no display of anger, she spoke, in short, broken sentences:

"She has been his mistress for the last four years. . . I can't tell you how I suffered. . . She herself told me of it. . . out of sheer wickedness. . . Her loathing for me was even greater than her love for Jacques. . . and every day I had some fresh injury to bear. . . She would ring me up to tell me of her appointments with my husband. . . she hoped to make me suffer so much I should end by killing myself. . . I did think of it sometimes, but I held out, for the children's sake. . . Jacques was weakening. She wanted him to get a divorce. . . and little by little he began to consent. . . dominated by her and by her brother, who is slyer than she is, but quite as dangerous. . . I felt all this. . . Jacques was becoming harsh to me. . . He had not the courage to leave me, but I was the obstacle and he bore me a grudge. . . Heavens, the tortures I suffered! . . ."

"You should have given him his liberty," cried Germaine Astaing. "A woman doesn't kill her husband for wanting a divorce."

Thérèse shook her head and answered:

"I did not kill him because he wanted a divorce. If he had really wanted it, he would have left me; and what could I have done? But your plans had changed, Germaine; divorce was not enough for you; and it was something else that you would have obtained from him, another, much more serious thing which you and your brother had insisted on. . . and to which he had consented. . . out of cowardice. . . in spite of himself. . ."

"What do you mean?" spluttered Germaine. "What other thing?"

"My death."

"You lie!" cried Madame Astaing.

Thérèse did not raise her voice. She made not a movement of aversion or indignation and simply repeated:

"My death, Germaine. I have read your latest letters, six letters from you which he was foolish enough to leave about in his pocket-book and which I read last night, six letters in which the terrible word is not set down, but in which it appears between every line. I trembled as I read it! That Jacques should come to this! . . . Nevertheless the idea of stabbing him did not occur to me for a second. A woman like myself, Germaine, does not readily commit murder. . . If I lost my head, it was after that. . . and it was your fault. . ."

She turned her eyes to Rénine as if to ask him if there was no danger in her speaking and revealing the truth.

"Don't be afraid," he said. "I will be answerable for everything."

She drew her hand across her forehead. The horrible scene was being reenacted within her and was torturing her. Germaine Astaing did not move, but stood with folded arms and anxious eyes, while Hortense Daniel sat distractedly awaiting the confession of the crime and the explanation of the unfathomable mystery.

"It was after that and it was through your fault Germaine. . . I had put back the pocket-book in the drawer where it was hidden; and I said nothing to Jacques this morning. . . I did not want to tell him what I knew. . . It was too horrible. . . All the same, I had to act quickly; your letters announced your secret arrival to-day. . . I thought at first of running away, of taking the train. . . I had mechanically picked up that dagger, to defend myself. . . But when Jacques and I went down to the beach, I was resigned. . . Yes, I had accepted death: 'I will die,' I thought, 'and put an end to all this nightmare!' . . . Only, for the children's sake, I was anxious that my death should look like an accident and that Jacques should have no part in it. That was why your plan of a walk on the cliff suited me. . . A fall from the top of a cliff seems quite natural. . . Jacques therefore left me to go to his cabin, from which he was to join you later at the Trois Mathildes. On the way, below the terrace, he dropped the key of the cabin. I went down and began to look for it with him. . . And it happened then. . . through your fault. . . yes, Germaine, through your fault. . . Jacques' pocket-book had slipped from his jacket, without his noticing it, and, together with the pocket-book, a photograph which I recognized at once: a photograph, taken this year, of myself and my two children. I picked it up. . . and I saw. . . You know what I saw, Germaine. Instead of my face, the face in the photograph was *yours*! . . . You had put in your likeness, Germaine, and blotted me out! It was your face! One of your arms was round my elder daughter's neck; and the younger was sitting on your knees. . . It was you, Germaine, the wife of my husband, the future mother of my children, you, who were going to bring them up. . . you, you! . . . Then I lost my head. I had the dagger. . . Jacques was stooping. . . I stabbed him. . ."

Every word of her confession was strictly true. Those who listened to her felt this profoundly; and nothing could have given Hortense and Rénine a keener impression of tragedy.

She had fallen back into her chair, utterly exhausted. Nevertheless, she went on speaking unintelligible words; and it was only gradually by leaning over her, that they were able to make out:

"I thought that there would be an outcry and that I should be arrested. But no. It happened in such a way and under such conditions that no one had seen anything. Further, Jacques had drawn himself up at the same time as myself; and he actually did not fall. No, he did not fall! I had stabbed him; and he remained standing! I saw him from the terrace, to which I had returned. He had hung his jacket over his shoulders, evidently to hide his wound, and he moved away without staggering. . . or staggering so little that I alone was able to perceive it. He even spoke to some friends who were playing cards. Then he went to his cabin and disappeared. . . In a few moments, I came back indoors. I was persuaded that all of this was only a bad dream. . . that I had not killed him. . . or that at the worst the wound was a slight one. Jacques would come out again. I was certain of it. . . I watched from my balcony. . . If I had thought for a moment that he needed assistance, I should have flown to him. . . But truly I didn't know. . . I didn't guess. . . People speak of presentiments: there are no such things. I was perfectly calm, just as one is after a nightmare of which the memory is fading away. . . No, I swear to you, I knew nothing. . . until the moment. . ."

She interrupted herself, stifled by sobs.

Rénine finished her sentence for her,

"Until the moment when they came and told you, I suppose?"

Thérèse stammered:

"Yes. It was not till then that I was conscious of what I had done. . . and I felt that I was going mad and that I should cry out to all those people, 'Why, it was I who did it! Don't search! Here is the dagger. . . I am the culprit!' Yes, I was going to say that, when suddenly I caught sight of my poor Jacques. . . They were carrying him along. . . His face was very peaceful, very gentle. . . And, in his presence, I understood my duty, as he had understood his. . . He had kept silent, for the sake of the children. I would be silent too. We were both guilty of the murder of which he was the victim; and we must both do all we could to prevent the crime from recoiling upon them. . . He had seen this clearly in his dying agony. He had had the amazing courage to keep his feet, to answer the people who spoke to him and to lock himself up to die. He had done this, wiping out all his faults with a single action, and in so doing had granted me his forgiveness, because he was not accusing me. . . and was ordering me to hold my peace. . . and to defend myself. . . against everybody. . . especially against you, Germaine."

She uttered these last words more firmly. At first wholly overwhelmed by the unconscious act which she had committed in killing her husband, she had recovered her strength a little in thinking of what she had done and in defending herself with such energy. Faced by the intriguing woman whose hatred had driven both of them to death and crime, she clenched her fists, ready for the struggle, all quivering with resolution.

Germaine Astaing did not flinch. She had listened without a word, with a relentless expression which grew harder and harder as Thérèse's confessions became precise. No emotion seemed to soften her and no remorse to penetrate her being. At most, towards the end, her thin lips shaped themselves into a faint smile. She was holding her prey in her clutches.

Slowly, with her eyes raised to a mirror, she adjusted her hat and powdered her face. Then she walked to the door.

Thérèse darted forward:

"Where are you going?"

"Where I choose."

"To see the examining-magistrate?"

"Very likely."

"You sha'n't pass!"

"As you please. I'll wait for him here."

"And you'll tell him what?"

"Why, all that you've said, of course, all that you've been silly enough to say. How could he doubt the story? You have explained it all to me so fully."

Thérèse took her by the shoulders:

"Yes, but I'll explain other things to him at the same time, Germaine, things that concern you. If I'm ruined, so shall you be."

"You can't touch me."

"I can expose you, show your letters."

"What letters?"

"Those in which my death was decided on."

"Lies, Thérèse! You know that famous plot exists only in your imagination. Neither Jacques nor I wished for your death."

"You did, at any rate. Your letters condemn you."

"Lies! They were the letters of a friend to a friend."

"Letters of a mistress to her paramour."

"Prove it."

"They are there, in Jacques' pocket-book."

"No, they're not."

"What's that you say?"

"I say that those letters belonged to me. I've taken them back, or rather my brother has."

"You've stolen them, you wretch! And you shall give them back again," cried Thérèse, shaking her.

"I haven't them. My brother kept them. He has gone."

Thérèse staggered and stretched out her hands to Rénine with an expression of despair. Rénine said:

"What she says is true. I watched the brother's proceedings while he was feeling in your bag. He took out the pocket-book, looked through it with his sister, came and put it back again and went off with the letters."

Rénine paused and added,

"Or, at least, with five of them."

The two women moved closer to him. What did he intend to convey? If Frédéric Astaing had taken away only five letters, what had become of the sixth?

"I suppose," said Rénine, "that, when the pocket-book fell on the shingle, that sixth letter slipped out at the same time as the photograph and that M. d'Ormeval must have picked it up, for I found it in the pocket of his blazer, which had been hung up near the bed. Here it is. It's signed Germaine Astaing and it is quite enough to prove the writer's intentions and the murderous counsels which she was pressing upon her lover."

Madame Astaing had turned grey in the face and was so much disconcerted that she did not try to defend herself. Rénine continued, addressing his remarks to her:

"To my mind, madame, you are responsible for all that happened. Penniless, no doubt, and at the end of your resources, you tried to profit by the passion with which you inspired M. d'Ormeval in order to make him marry you, in spite of all the obstacles, and to lay your hands upon his fortune. I have proofs of this greed for money and these abominable calculations and can supply them if need be. A few minutes after I had felt in the pocket of that jacket, you did the same. I had removed the sixth letter, but had left a slip of paper which you looked for eagerly and which also must have dropped out of the pocket-book. It was an uncrossed cheque for a hundred thousand francs, drawn by M. d'Ormeval in your brother's name. . . just a little wedding-present. . . what we might call pin-money. Acting on your instructions, your brother dashed off by motor to Le Havre to reach the bank before four o'clock. I may as well tell you that he will not have cashed the cheque, for I had a telephone-message sent to the bank to announce the murder of M. d'Ormeval, which stops all payments. The upshot of all this is that the police, if you persist in your schemes of revenge, will have in their hands all the proofs that are wanted against you and your brother. I might add, as an edifying piece of evidence, the story of the conversation which I overheard between your brother and yourself in a dining-car on the railway between Brest and Paris, a fortnight ago. But I feel sure that you will not drive me to adopt these extreme measures and that we understand each other. Isn't that so?"

Natures like Madame Astaing's, which are violent and headstrong so long as a fight is possible and while a gleam of hope remains, are easily swayed in defeat. Germaine was too intelligent not to grasp the fact that the least attempt at resistance would be shattered by such an adversary as this. She was in his hands. She could but yield.

She therefore did not indulge in any play-acting, nor in any demonstration such as threats, outbursts of fury or hysterics. She bowed:

"We are agreed," she said. "What are your terms?"

"Go away. If ever you are called upon for your evidence, say that you know nothing."

She walked away. At the door, she hesitated and then, between her teeth, said:

"The cheque."

Rénine looked at Madame d'Ormeval, who declared:

"Let her keep it. I would not touch that money."

When Rénine had given Thérèse d'Ormeval precise instructions as to how she was to behave at the enquiry and to answer the questions put to her, he left the chalet, accompanied by Hortense Daniel.

On the beach below, the magistrate and the public prosecutor were continuing their investigations, taking measurements, examining the witnesses and generally laying their heads together.

"When I think," said Hortense, "that you have the dagger and M. d'Ormeval's pocket-book on you!"

"And it strikes you as awfully dangerous, I suppose?" he said, laughing. "It strikes *me* as awfully comic."

"Aren't you afraid?"

"Of what?"

"That they may suspect something?"

"Lord, they won't suspect a thing! We shall tell those good people what we saw and our evidence will only increase their perplexity, for we saw nothing at all. For prudence sake we will stay a day or two, to see which way the wind is blowing. But it's quite settled: they will never be able to make head or tail of the matter."

"Nevertheless, *you* guessed the secret and from the first. Why?"

"Because, instead of seeking difficulties where none exist, as people generally do, I always put the question as it should be put; and the solution comes quite naturally. A man goes to his cabin and locks himself in. Half an hour later, he is found inside, dead. No one has gone in. What has happened? To my mind there is only one answer. There is no need to think about it. As the murder was not committed in the cabin, it must have been committed beforehand and the man was already mortally wounded when he entered his cabin. And forthwith the truth in this particular case appeared to me. Madame d'Ormeval, who was to have been killed this evening, forestalled her murderers and while her husband was stooping to the ground, in a moment of frenzy stabbed him in the back. There was nothing left to do but look for the reasons that prompted her action. When I knew them, I took her part unreservedly. That's the whole story."

The day was beginning to wane. The blue of the sky was becoming darker and the sea, even more peaceful than before.

"What are you thinking of?" asked Rénine, after a moment.

"I am thinking," she said, "that if I too were the victim of some machination, I should trust you whatever happened, trust you through and against all. I know, as certainly as I know that I exist, that you would save me, whatever the obstacles might be. There is no limit to the power of your will."

He said, very softly:

"There is no limit to my wish to please you."

VI

The Lady with the Hatchet

One of the most incomprehensible incidents that preceded the great war was certainly the one which was known as the episode of the lady with the hatchet. The solution of the mystery was unknown and would never have been known, had not circumstances in the cruellest fashion obliged Prince Rénine—or should I say, Arsène Lupin?—to take up the matter and had I not been able to-day to tell the true story from the details supplied by him.

Let me recite the facts. In a space of eighteen months, five women disappeared, five women of different stations in life, all between twenty and thirty years of age and living in Paris or the Paris district.

I will give their names: Madame Ladoue, the wife of a doctor; Mlle. Ardant, the daughter of a banker; Mlle. Covereau, a washer-woman of Courbevoie; Mlle. Honorine Vernisset, a dressmaker; and Madame Grollinger, an artist. These five women disappeared without the possibility of discovering a single particular to explain why they had left their homes, why they did not return to them, who had enticed them away, and where and how they were detained.

Each of these women, a week after her departure, was found somewhere or other in the western outskirts of Paris; and each time it was a dead body that was found, the dead body of a woman who had been killed by a blow on the head from a hatchet. And each time, not far from the woman, who was firmly bound, her face covered with blood and her body emaciated by lack of food, the marks of carriage-wheels proved that the corpse had been driven to the spot.

The five murders were so much alike that there was only a single investigation, embracing all the five enquiries and, for that matter, leading to no result. A woman disappeared; a week later, to a day, her body was discovered; and that was all. The bonds that fastened her were similar in each case; so were the tracks left by the wheels; so were the blows of the hatchet, all of which were struck vertically at the top and right in the middle of the forehead.

The motive of the crime? The five women had been completely stripped of their jewels, purses and other objects of value. But the robberies might well have been attributed to marauders or any passersby, since the bodies were lying in deserted spots. Were the authorities to believe in the execution of a plan of revenge or of a plan intended to do away with the series of persons mutually connected, persons, for instance, likely to benefit by a future inheritance? Here again the same obscurity prevailed. Theories were built up, only to be demolished forthwith by an examination of the facts. Trails were followed and at once abandoned.

And suddenly there was a sensation. A woman engaged in sweeping the roads picked up on the pavement a little note-book which she brought to the local police-station. The leaves of this note-book were all blank, excepting one, on which was written a list of the murdered women, with their names set down in order of date and accompanied by three figures: Ladoue, 132; Vernisset, 118; and so on.

Certainly no importance would have been attached to these entries, which anybody might have written, since every one was acquainted with the sinister list. But, instead of five names, it included six! Yes, below the words "Grollinger, 128," there appeared "Williamson, 114." Did this indicate a sixth murder?

The obviously English origin of the name limited the field of the investigations, which did not in fact take long. It was ascertained that, a fortnight ago, a Miss Hermione Williamson, a governess in a family at Auteuil, had left her place to go back to England and that, since then, her sisters, though she had written to tell them that she was coming over, had heard no more of her.

A fresh enquiry was instituted. A postman found the body in the Meudon woods. Miss Williamson's skull was split down the middle.

I need not describe the public excitement at this stage nor the shudder of horror which passed through the crowd when it read this list, written without a doubt in the murderer's own hand. What could be more frightful than such a record, kept up to date like a careful tradesman's ledger:

"On such a day, I killed so-and-so; on such a day so-and-so!"

And the sum total was six dead bodies.

Against all expectation, the experts in handwriting had no difficulty in agreeing and unanimously declared that the writing was "that of a woman, an educated woman, possessing artistic tastes, imagination and an extremely sensitive nature." The "lady with the hatchet," as the journalists christened her, was decidedly no ordinary person;

and scores of newspaper-articles made a special study of her case, exposing her mental condition and losing themselves in far-fetched explanations.

Nevertheless it was the writer of one of these articles, a young journalist whose chance discovery made him the centre of public attention, who supplied the one element of truth and shed upon the darkness the only ray of light that was to penetrate it. In casting about for the meaning of the figures which followed the six names, he had come to ask himself whether those figures did not simply represent the number of the days separating one crime from the next. All that he had to do was to check the dates. He at once found that his theory was correct. Mlle. Vernisset had been carried off one hundred and thirty-two days after Madame Ladoue; Mlle. Covereau one hundred and eighteen days after Honorine Vernisset; and so on.

There was therefore no room for doubt; and the police had no choice but to accept a solution which so precisely fitted the circumstances: the figures corresponded with the intervals. There was no mistake in the records of the lady with the hatchet.

But then one deduction became inevitable. Miss Williamson, the latest victim, had been carried off on the 26th of June last, and her name was followed by the figures 114: was it not to be presumed that a fresh crime would be committed a hundred and fourteen days later, that is to say, on the 18th of October? Was it not probable that the horrible business would be repeated in accordance with the murderer's secret intentions? Were they not bound to pursue to its logical conclusion the argument which ascribed to the figures—to all the figures, to the last as well as to the others—their value as eventual dates?

Now it was precisely this deduction which was drawn and was being weighed and discussed during the few days that preceded the 18th of October, when logic demanded the performance of yet another act of the abominable tragedy. And it was only natural that, on the morning of that day, Prince Rénine and Hortense, when making an appointment by telephone for the evening, should allude to the newspaper-articles which they had both been reading:

"Look out!" said Rénine, laughing. "If you meet the lady with the hatchet, take the other side of the road!"

"And, if the good lady carries me off, what am I to do?"

"Strew your path with little white pebbles and say, until the very moment when the hatchet flashes in the air, 'I have nothing to fear; *he* will save me.' *He* is myself. . . and I kiss your hands. Till this evening, my dear."

That afternoon, Rénine had an appointment with Rose Andrée and Dalbrèque to arrange for their departure for the States.* Before four and seven o'clock, he bought the different editions of the evening papers. None of them reported an abduction.

At nine o'clock he went to the Gymnase, where he had taken a private box.

At half-past nine, as Hortense had not arrived, he rang her up, though without thought of anxiety. The maid replied that Madame Daniel had not come in yet.

Seized with a sudden fear, Rénine hurried to the furnished flat which Hortense was occupying for the time being, near the Parc Monceau, and questioned the maid, whom he had engaged for her and who was completely devoted to him. The woman said that her mistress had gone out at two o'clock, with a stamped letter in her hand, saying that she was going to the post and that she would come back to dress. This was the last that had been seen of her.

"To whom was the letter addressed?"

"To you, sir. I saw the writing on the envelope: Prince Serge Rénine."

He waited until midnight, but in vain. Hortense did not return; nor did she return next day.

"Not a word to any one," said Rénine to the maid. "Say that your mistress is in the country and that you are going to join her."

For his own part, he had not a doubt: Hortense's disappearance was explained by the very fact of the date, the 18th of October. She was the seventh victim of the lady with the hatchet.

"The abduction," said Rénine to himself, "precedes the blow of the hatchet by a week. I have, therefore, at the present moment, seven full days before me. Let us say six, to avoid any surprise. This is Saturday: Hortense must be set free by mid-day on Friday; and, to make sure of this, I must know her hiding-place by nine o'clock on Thursday evening at latest."

Rénine wrote, "Thursday Evening, Nine O'Clock," in big letters, on a card which he nailed above the mantelpiece in his study. Then at midday on Saturday, the day after the disappearance, he locked himself

---

* See *The Tell-tale Film.*

into the study, after telling his man not to disturb him except for meals and letters.

He spent four days there, almost without moving. He had immediately sent for a set of all the leading newspapers which had spoken in detail of the first six crimes. When he had read and reread them, he closed the shutters, drew the curtains and lay down on the sofa in the dark, with the door bolted, thinking.

By Tuesday evening he was no further advanced than on the Saturday. The darkness was as dense as ever. He had not discovered the smallest clue for his guidance, nor could he see the slightest reason to hope.

At times, notwithstanding his immense power of self-control and his unlimited confidence in the resources at his disposal, at times he would quake with anguish. Would he arrive in time? There was no reason why he should see more clearly during the last few days than during those which had already elapsed. And this meant that Hortense Daniel would inevitably be murdered.

The thought tortured him. He was attached to Hortense by a much stronger and deeper feeling than the appearance of the relations between them would have led an onlooker to believe. The curiosity at the beginning, the first desire, the impulse to protect Hortense, to distract her, to inspire her with a relish for existence: all this had simply turned to love. Neither of them was aware of it, because they barely saw each other save at critical times when they were occupied with the adventures of others and not with their own. But, at the first onslaught of danger, Rénine realized the place which Hortense had taken in his life and he was in despair at knowing her to be a prisoner and a martyr and at being unable to save her.

He spent a feverish, agitated night, turning the case over and over from every point of view. The Wednesday morning was also a terrible time for him. He was losing ground. Giving up his hermit-like seclusion, he threw open the windows and paced to and fro through his rooms, ran out into the street and came in again, as though fleeing before the thought that obsessed him:

"Hortense is suffering. . . Hortense is in the depths. . . She sees the hatchet. . . She is calling to me. . . She is entreating me. . . And I can do nothing. . ."

It was at five o'clock in the afternoon that, on examining the list of the six names, he received that little inward shock which is a sort of signal of the truth that is being sought for. A light shot through his mind. It was not, to be sure, that brilliant light in which every detail is made plain, but it was enough to tell him in which direction to move.

His plan of campaign was formed at once. He sent Adolphe, his chauffeur, to the principal newspapers, with a few lines which were to appear in type among the next morning's advertisements. Adolphe was also told to go to the laundry at Courbevoie, where Mlle. Covereau, the second of the six victims, had been employed.

On the Thursday, Rénine did not stir out of doors. In the afternoon, he received several letters in reply to his advertisement. Then two telegrams arrived. Lastly, at three o'clock, there came a pneumatic letter, bearing the Trocadéro postmark, which seemed to be what he was expecting.

He turned up a directory, noted an address—"M. de Lourtier-Vaneau, retired colonial governor, 47 *bis*, Avenue Kléber"—and ran down to his car:

"Adolphe, 47 *bis*, Avenue Kléber."

H E   W A S   S H O W N   I N T O   A large study furnished with magnificent book-cases containing old volumes in costly bindings. M. de Lourtier-Vaneau was a man still in the prime of life, wearing a slightly grizzled beard and, by his affable manners and genuine distinction, commanding confidence and liking.

"M. de Lourtier," said Rénine, "I have ventured to call on your excellency because I read in last year's newspapers that you used to know one of the victims of the lady with the hatchet, Honorine Vernisset."

"Why, of course we knew her!" cried M. de Lourtier. "My wife used to employ her as a dressmaker by the day. Poor girl!"

"M. de Lourtier, a lady of my acquaintance has disappeared as the other six victims disappeared."

"What!" exclaimed M. de Lourtier, with a start. "But I have followed the newspapers carefully. There was nothing on the 18th of October."

"Yes, a woman of whom I am very fond, Madame Hortense Daniel, was abducted on the 17th of October."

"And this is the 22nd!"

"Yes; and the murder will be committed on the 24th."

"Horrible! Horrible! It must be prevented at all costs. . ."

"And I shall perhaps succeed in preventing it, with your excellency's assistance."

"But have you been to the police?"

"No. We are faced by mysteries which are, so to speak, absolute and compact, which offer no gap through which the keenest eyes can see and which it is useless to hope to clear up by ordinary methods, such as inspection of the scenes of the crimes, police enquiries, searching for finger-prints and so on. As none of those proceedings served any good purpose in the previous cases, it would be waste of time to resort to them in a seventh, similar case. An enemy who displays such skill and subtlety would not leave behind her any of those clumsy traces which are the first things that a professional detective seizes upon."

"Then what have you done?"

"Before taking any action, I have reflected. I gave four days to thinking the matter over."

M. de Lourtier-Vaneau examined his visitor closely and, with a touch of irony, asked:

"And the result of your meditations. . . ?"

"To begin with," said Rénine, refusing to be put out of countenance, "I have submitted all these cases to a comprehensive survey, which hitherto no one else had done. This enabled me to discover their general meaning, to put aside all the tangle of embarrassing theories and, since no one was able to agree as to the motives of all this filthy business, to attribute it to the only class of persons capable of it."

"That is to say?"

"Lunatics, your excellency."

M. de Lourtier-Vaneau started:

"Lunatics? What an idea!"

"M. de Lourtier, the woman known as the lady with the hatchet is a madwoman."

"But she would be locked up!"

"We don't know that she's not. We don't know that she is not one of those half-mad people, apparently harmless, who are watched so slightly that they have full scope to indulge their little manias, their wild-beast instincts. Nothing could be more treacherous than these creatures. Nothing could be more crafty, more patient, more persistent, more dangerous and at the same time more absurd and more logical, more slovenly and more methodical. All these epithets, M. de Lourtier, may be applied to the doings of the lady with the hatchet. The obsession of an idea and the continual repetition of an act are characteristics of the maniac. I do not yet know the idea by which the lady with the hatchet is obsessed but I do know the act that results from it; and it is always the same. The victim is bound with precisely similar ropes. She is killed after the same number of days. She is struck by an identical blow, with the same instrument, in the same place, the middle of the forehead, producing an absolutely vertical wound. An ordinary murderer displays some variety. His trembling hand swerves aside and strikes awry. The lady with the hatchet does not tremble. It is as though she had taken measurements; and the edge of her weapon does not swerve by a hair's breadth. Need I give you any further proofs or examine all the other details with you? Surely not. You now possess the key to the riddle; and you know as I do that only a lunatic can behave in this way, stupidly, savagely, mechanically, like a striking clock or the blade of the guillotine. . ."

M. de Lourtier-Vaneau nodded his head:

"Yes, that is so. One can see the whole affair from that angle. . . and I am beginning to believe that this is how one ought to see it. But, if we admit that this madwoman has the sort of mathematical logic which governed the murders of the six victims, I see no connection between the victims themselves. She struck at random. Why this victim rather than that?"

"Ah," said Rénine. "Your excellency is asking me a question which I asked myself from the first moment, the question which sums up the whole problem and which cost me so much trouble to solve! Why Hortense Daniel rather than another? Among two millions of women who might have been selected, why Hortense? Why little Vernisset? Why Miss Williamson? If the affair is such as I conceived it, as a whole, that is to say, based upon the blind and fantastic logic of a madwoman, a choice was inevitably exercised. Now in what did that choice consist? What was the quality, or the defect, or the sign needed to induce the lady with the hatchet to strike? In a word, if she chose—and she must have chosen— what directed her choice?"

"Have you found the answer?"

Rénine paused and replied:

"Yes, your excellency, I have. And I could have found it at the very outset, since all that I had to do was to make a careful examination of the list of victims. But these flashes of truth are never kindled save in a brain overstimulated by effort and reflection. I stared at the list twenty times over, before that little detail took a definite shape."

"I don't follow you," said M. de Lourtier-Vaneau.

"M. de Lourtier, it may be noted that, if a number of persons are brought together in any transaction, or crime, or public scandal or what not, they are almost invariably described in the same way. On this occasion, the newspapers never mentioned anything more than their surnames in speaking of Madame Ladoue, Mlle. Ardent or Mlle. Covereau. On the other hand, Mlle. Vernisset and Miss Williamson were always described by their Christian names as well: Honorine and Hermione. If the same thing had been done in the case of all the six victims, there would have been no mystery."

"Why not?"

"Because we should at once have realized the relation existing between the six unfortunate women, as I myself suddenly realized it on comparing those two Christian names with that of Hortense Daniel. You understand now, don't you? You see the three Christian names before your eyes. . ."

M. de Lourtier-Vaneau seemed to be perturbed. Turning a little pale, he said:

"What do you mean? What do you mean?"

"I mean," continued Rénine, in a clear voice, sounding each syllable separately, "I mean that you see before your eyes three Christian names which all three begin with the same initial and which all three, by a remarkable coincidence, consist of the same number of letters, as you may prove. If you enquire at the Courbevoie laundry, where Mlle. Covereau used to work, you will find that her name was Hilairie. Here again we have the same initial and the same number of letters. There is no need to seek any farther. We are sure, are we not, that the Christian names of all the victims offer the same peculiarities? And this gives us, with absolute certainty, the key to the problem which was set us. It explains the madwoman's choice. We now know the connection between the unfortunate victims. There can be no mistake about it. It's that and nothing else. And how this method of choosing confirms my theory! What proof of madness! Why kill these women rather than any others? Because their names begin with an H and consist of eight letters! You understand me, M. de Lourtier, do you not? The number of letters is eight. The initial letter is the eighth letter of the alphabet; and the word *huit*, eight, begins with an H. Always the letter H. *And the implement used to commit the crime was a hatchet.* Is your excellency prepared to tell me that the lady with the hatchet is not a madwoman?"

Rénine interrupted himself and went up to M. de Lourtier-Vaneau:

"What's the matter, your excellency? Are you unwell?"

"No, no," said M. de Lourtier, with the perspiration streaming down his forehead. "No. . . but all this story is so upsetting! Only think, I knew one of the victims! And then. . ."

Rénine took a water-bottle and tumbler from a small table, filled the glass and handed it to M. de Lourtier, who sipped a few mouthfuls from it and then, pulling himself together, continued, in a voice which he strove to make firmer than it had been:

"Very well. We'll admit your supposition. Even so, it is necessary that it should lead to tangible results. What have you done?"

"This morning I published in all the newspapers an advertisement worded as follows: 'Excellent cook seeks situation. Write before 5 P.M. to Herminie, Boulevard Haussmann, etc.' You continue to follow me, don't you, M. de Lourtier? Christian names beginning with an H and consisting of eight letters are extremely rare and are all rather out of date: Herminie, Hilairie, Hermione. Well, these Christian names, for reasons which I do not understand, are essential to the madwoman. She cannot do without them. To find women bearing one of these Christian names and for this purpose only she summons up all her remaining powers of reason, discernment, reflection and intelligence. She hunts about. She asks questions. She lies in wait. She reads newspapers which she hardly understands, but in which certain details, certain capital letters catch her eye. And consequently I did not doubt for a second that this name of Herminie, printed in large type, would attract her attention and that she would be caught to-day in the trap of my advertisement."

"Did she write?" asked M. de Lourtier-Vaneau, anxiously.

"Several ladies," Rénine continued, "wrote the letters which are usual in such cases, to offer a home to the so-called Herminie. But I received an express letter which struck me as interesting."

"From whom?"

"Read it, M. de Lourtier."

M. de Lourtier-Vaneau snatched the sheet from Rénine's hands and cast a glance at the signature. His first movement was one of surprise, as though he had expected something different. Then he gave a long, loud laugh of something like joy and relief.

"Why do you laugh, M. de Lourtier? You seem pleased."

"Pleased, no. But this letter is signed by my wife."

"And you were afraid of finding something else?"

"Oh no! But since it's my wife. . ."

He did not finish his sentence and said to Rénine:

"Come this way."

He led him through a passage to a little drawing-room where a fair-haired lady, with a happy and tender expression on her comely face, was sitting in the midst of three children and helping them with their lessons.

She rose. M. de Lourtier briefly presented his visitor and asked his wife:

"Suzanne, is this express message from you?"

"To Mlle. Herminie, Boulevard Haussmann? Yes," she said, "I sent it. As you know, our parlour-maid's leaving and I'm looking out for a new one."

Rénine interrupted her:

"Excuse me, madame. Just one question: where did you get the woman's address?"

She flushed. Her husband insisted:

"Tell us, Suzanne. Who gave you the address?"

"I was rung up."

"By whom?"

She hesitated and then said:

"Your old nurse."

"Félicienne?"

"Yes."

M. de Lourtier cut short the conversation and, without permitting Rénine to ask any more questions, took him back to the study:

"You see, monsieur, that pneumatic letter came from a quite natural source. Félicienne, my old nurse, who lives not far from Paris on an allowance which I make her, read your advertisement and told Madame de Lourtier of it. For, after all," he added laughing, "I don't suppose that you suspect my wife of being the lady with the hatchet."

"No."

"Then the incident is closed. . . at least on my side. I have done what I could, I have listened to your arguments and I am very sorry that I can be of no more use to you. . ."

He drank another glass of water and sat down. His face was distorted. Rénine looked at him for a few seconds, as a man will look at a failing adversary who has only to receive the knock-out blow, and, sitting down beside him, suddenly gripped his arm:

"Your excellency, if you do not speak, Hortense Daniel will be the seventh victim."

"I have nothing to say, monsieur! What do you think I know?"

"The truth! My explanations have made it plain to you. Your distress, your terror are positive proofs."

"But, after all, monsieur, if I knew, why should I be silent?"

"For fear of scandal. There is in your life, so a profound intuition assures me, something that you are constrained to hide. The truth about this monstrous tragedy, which suddenly flashed upon you, this truth, if it were known, would spell dishonour to you, disgrace. . . and you are shrinking from your duty."

M. de Lourtier did not reply. Rénine leant over him and, looking him in the eyes, whispered:

"There will be no scandal. I shall be the only person in the world to know what has happened. And I am as much interested as yourself in not attracting attention, because I love Hortense Daniel and do not wish her name to be mixed up in your horrible story."

They remained face to face during a long interval. Rénine's expression was harsh and unyielding. M. de Lourtier felt that nothing would bend him if the necessary words remained unspoken; but he could not bring himself to utter them:

"You are mistaken," he said. "You think you have seen things that don't exist."

Rénine received a sudden and terrifying conviction that, if this man took refuge in a stolid silence, there was no hope for Hortense Daniel; and he was so much infuriated by the thought that the key to the riddle lay there, within reach of his hand, that he clutched M. de Lourtier by the throat and forced him backwards:

"I'll have no more lies! A woman's life is at stake! Speak. . . and speak at once! If not. . . !"

M. de Lourtier had no strength left in him. All resistance was impossible. It was not that Rénine's attack alarmed him, or that he was yielding to this act of violence, but he felt crushed by that indomitable will, which seemed to admit no obstacle, and he stammered:

"You are right. It is my duty to tell everything, whatever comes of it."

"Nothing will come of it, I pledge my word, on condition that you save Hortense Daniel. A moment's hesitation may undo us all. Speak. No details, but the actual facts."

"Madame de Lourtier is not my wife. The only woman who has the right to bear my name is one whom I married when I was a young colonial official. She was a rather eccentric woman, of feeble mentality and incredibly subject to impulses that amounted to monomania. We had two children, twins, whom she worshipped and in whose company she would no doubt have recovered her mental balance and moral health, when, by a stupid accident—a passing carriage—they were killed before her eyes. The poor thing went mad. . . with the silent, secretive madness which you imagined. Some time afterwards, when I was appointed to an Algerian station, I brought her to France and put her in the charge of a worthy creature who had nursed me and brought me up. Two years later, I made the acquaintance of the woman who was to become the joy of my life. You saw her just now. She is the mother of my children and she passes as my wife. Are we to sacrifice her? Is our whole existence to be shipwrecked in horror and must our name be coupled with this tragedy of madness and blood?"

Rénine thought for a moment and asked:

"What is the other one's name?"

"Hermance."

"Hermance! Still that initial. . . still those eight letters!"

"That was what made me realize everything just now," said M. de Lourtier. "When you compared the different names, I at once reflected that my unhappy wife was called Hermance and that she was mad. . . and all the proofs leapt to my mind."

"But, though we understand the selection of the victims, how are we to explain the murders? What are the symptoms of her madness? Does she suffer at all?"

"She does not suffer very much at present. But she has suffered in the past, the most terrible suffering that you can imagine: since the moment when her two children were run over before her eyes, night and day she had the horrible spectacle of their death before her eyes, without a moment's interruption, for she never slept for a single second. Think of the torture of it! To see her children dying through all the hours of the long day and all the hours of the interminable night!"

"Nevertheless," Rénine objected, "it is not to drive away that picture that she commits murder?"

"Yes, possibly," said M. de Lourtier, thoughtfully, "to drive it away by sleep."

"I don't understand."

"You don't understand, because we are talking of a madwoman. . . and because all that happens in that disordered brain is necessarily incoherent and abnormal?"

"Obviously. But, all the same, is your supposition based on facts that justify it?"

"Yes, on facts which I had, in a way, overlooked but which to-day assume their true significance. The first of these facts dates a few years back, to a morning when my old nurse for the first time found Hermance fast asleep. Now she was holding her hands clutched around a puppy which she had strangled. And the same thing was repeated on three other occasions."

"And she slept?"

"Yes, each time she slept a sleep which lasted for several nights."

"And what conclusion did you draw?"

"I concluded that the relaxation of the nerves provoked by taking life exhausted her and predisposed her for sleep."

Rénine shuddered:

"That's it! There's not a doubt of it! The taking life, the effort of killing makes her sleep. And she began with women what had served her so well with animals. All her madness has become concentrated on that one point: she kills them to rob them of their sleep! She wanted sleep; and she steals the sleep of others! That's it, isn't it? For the past two years, she has been sleeping?"

"For the past two years, she has been sleeping," stammered M. de Lourtier.

Rénine gripped him by the shoulder:

"And it never occurred to you that her madness might go farther, that she would stop at nothing to win the blessing of sleep! Let us make haste, monsieur! All this is horrible!"

They were both making for the door, when M. de Lourtier hesitated. The telephone-bell was ringing.

"It's from there," he said.

"From there?"

"Yes, my old nurse gives me the news at the same time every day."

He unhooked the receivers and handed one to Rénine, who whispered in his ear the questions which he was to put.

"Is that you, Félicienne? How is she?"

"Not so bad, sir."

"Is she sleeping well?"

"Not very well, lately. Last night, indeed, she never closed her eyes. So she's very gloomy just now."

"What is she doing at the moment?"

"She is in her room."

"Go to her, Félicienne, and don't leave her."

"I can't. She's locked herself in."

"You must, Félicienne. Break open the door. I'm coming straight on. . . Hullo! Hullo! . . . Oh, damnation, they've cut us off!"

Without a word, the two men left the flat and ran down to the avenue. Rénine hustled M. de Lourtier into the car:

"What address?"

"Ville d'Avray."

"Of course! In the very center of her operations. . . like a spider in the middle of her web! Oh, the shame of it!"

He was profoundly agitated. He saw the whole adventure in its monstrous reality.

"Yes, she kills them to steal their sleep, as she used to kill the animals. It is the same obsession, but complicated by a whole array of utterly incomprehensible practices and superstitions. She evidently fancies that the similarity of the Christian names to her own is indispensable and that she will not sleep unless her victim is an Hortense or an Honorine. It's a madwoman's argument; its logic escapes us and we know nothing of its origin; but we can't get away from it. She has to hunt and has to find. And she finds and carries off her prey beforehand and watches over it for the appointed number of days, until the moment when, crazily, through the hole which she digs with a hatchet in the middle of the skull, she absorbs the sleep which stupefies her and grants her oblivion for a given period. And here again we see absurdity and madness. Why does she fix that period at so many days? Why should one victim ensure her a hundred and twenty days of sleep and another a hundred and twenty-five? What insanity! The calculation is mysterious and of course mad; but the fact remains that, at the end of a hundred or a hundred and twenty-five days, as the case may be, a fresh victim is sacrificed; and there have been six already and the seventh is awaiting her turn. Ah, monsieur, what a terrible responsibility for you! Such a monster as that! She should never have been allowed out of sight!"

M. de Lourtier-Vaneau made no protest. His air of dejection, his pallor, his trembling hands, all proved his remorse and his despair: "She deceived me," he murmured. "She was outwardly so quiet, so docile! And, after all, she's in a lunatic asylum."

"Then how can she. . . ?"

"The asylum," explained M. de Lourtier, "is made up of a number of separate buildings scattered over extensive grounds. The sort of cottage in which Hermance lives stands quite apart. There is first a room occupied by Félicienne, then Hermance's bedroom and two separate rooms, one of which has its windows overlooking the open country. I suppose it is there that she locks up her victims."

"But the carriage that conveys the dead bodies?"

"The stables of the asylum are quite close to the cottage. There's a horse and carriage there for station work. Hermance no doubt gets up at night, harnesses the horse and slips the body through the window."

"And the nurse who watches her?"

"Félicienne is very old and rather deaf."

"But by day she sees her mistress moving to and fro, doing this and that. Must we not admit a certain complicity?"

"Never! Félicienne herself has been deceived by Hermance's hypocrisy."

"All the same, it was she who telephoned to Madame de Lourtier first, about that advertisement. . ."

"Very naturally. Hermance, who talks now and then, who argues, who buries herself in the newspapers, which she does not understand, as you were saying just now, but reads through them attentively, must have seen the advertisement and, having heard that we were looking for a servant, must have asked Félicienne to ring me up."

"Yes. . . yes. . . that is what I felt," said Rénine, slowly. "She marks down her victims. . . With Hortense dead, she would have known, once she had used up her allowance of sleep, where to find an eighth victim. . . But how did she entice the unfortunate women? How did she entice Hortense?"

The car was rushing along, but not fast enough to please Rénine, who rated the chauffeur:

"Push her along, Adolphe, can't you? . . . We're losing time, my man."

Suddenly the fear of arriving too late began to torture him. The logic of the insane is subject to sudden changes of mood, to any perilous idea that may enter the mind. The madwoman might easily mistake the date and hasten the catastrophe, like a clock out of order which strikes an hour too soon.

On the other hand, as her sleep was once more disturbed, might she not be tempted to take action without waiting for the appointed moment? Was this not the reason why she had locked herself into her room? Heavens, what agonies her prisoner must be suffering! What shudders of terror at the executioner's least movement!

"Faster, Adolphe, or I'll take the wheel myself! Faster, hang it."

At last they reached Ville d'Avray. There was a steep, sloping road on the right and walls interrupted by a long railing.

"Drive round the grounds, Adolphe. We mustn't give warning of our presence, must we, M. de Lourtier? Where is the cottage?"

"Just opposite," said M. de Lourtier-Vaneau.

They got out a little farther on. Rénine began to run along a bank at the side of an ill-kept sunken road. It was almost dark. M. de Lourtier said:

"Here, this building standing a little way back. . . Look at that window on the ground-floor. It belongs to one of the separate rooms. . . and that is obviously how she slips out."

"But the window seems to be barred."

"Yes; and that is why no one suspected anything. But she must have found some way to get through."

The ground-floor was built over deep cellars. Rénine quickly clambered up, finding a foothold on a projecting ledge of stone.

Sure enough, one of the bars was missing.

He pressed his face to the window-pane and looked in.

The room was dark inside. Nevertheless he was able to distinguish at the back a woman seated beside another woman, who was lying on a mattress. The woman seated was holding her forehead in her hands and gazing at the woman who was lying down.

"It's she," whispered M. de Lourtier, who had also climbed the wall. "The other one is bound."

Rénine took from his pocket a glazier's diamond and cut out one of the panes without making enough noise to arouse the madwoman's attention. He next slid his hand to the window-fastening and turned it softly, while with his left hand he levelled a revolver.

"You're not going to fire, surely!" M. de Lourtier-Vaneau entreated.

"If I must, I shall."

Rénine pushed open the window gently. But there was an obstacle of which he was not aware, a chair which toppled over and fell.

He leapt into the room and threw away his revolver in order to seize the madwoman. But she did not wait for him. She rushed to the door, opened it and fled, with a hoarse cry.

M. de Lourtier made as though to run after her.

MAURICE LEBLANC

"What's the use?" said Rénine, kneeling down, "Let's save the victim first."

He was instantly reassured: Hortense was alive.

The first thing that he did was to cut the cords and remove the gag that was stifling her. Attracted by the noise, the old nurse had hastened to the room with a lamp, which Rénine took from her, casting its light on Hortense.

He was astounded: though livid and exhausted, with emaciated features and eyes blazing with fever, Hortense was trying to smile. She whispered:

"I was expecting you. . . I did not despair for a moment. . . I was sure of you. . ."

She fainted.

An hour later, after much useless searching around the cottage, they found the madwoman locked into a large cupboard in the loft. She had hanged herself.

HORTENSE REFUSED TO STAY ANOTHER night. Besides, it was better that the cottage should be empty when the old nurse announced the madwoman's suicide. Rénine gave Félicienne minute directions as to what she should do and say; and then, assisted by the chauffeur and M. de Lourtier, carried Hortense to the car and brought her home.

She was soon convalescent. Two days later, Rénine carefully questioned her and asked her how she had come to know the madwoman.

"It was very simple," she said. "My husband, who is not quite sane, as I have told you, is being looked after at Ville d'Avray; and I sometimes go to see him, without telling anybody, I admit. That was how I came to speak to that poor madwoman and how, the other day, she made signs that she wanted me to visit her. We were alone. I went into the cottage. She threw herself upon me and overpowered me before I had time to cry for help. I thought it was a jest; and so it was, wasn't it: a madwoman's jest? She was quite gentle with me. . . All the same, she let me starve. But I was so sure of you!"

"And weren't you frightened?"

"Of starving? No. Besides, she gave me some food, now and then, when the fancy took her. . . And then I was sure of you!"

"Yes, but there was something else: that other peril. . ."

"What other peril?" she asked, ingenuously.

Rénine gave a start. He suddenly understood—it seemed strange at first, though it was quite natural—that Hortense had not for a moment suspected and did not yet suspect the terrible danger which she had run. Her mind had not connected with her own adventure the murders committed by the lady with the hatchet.

He thought that it would always be time enough to tell her the truth. For that matter, a few days later her husband, who had been locked up for years, died in the asylum at Ville d'Avray, and Hortense, who had been recommended by her doctor a short period of rest and solitude, went to stay with a relation living near the village of Bassicourt, in the centre of France.

VII

Footprints in the Snow

To Prince Serge Rénine,
Boulevard Haussmann,
Paris

La Roncière
Near Bassicourt,
14 November.

My Dear Friend,—

"You must be thinking me very ungrateful. I have been here three weeks; and you have had not one letter from me! Not a word of thanks! And yet I ended by realizing from what terrible death you saved me and understanding the secret of that terrible business! But indeed, indeed I couldn't help it! I was in such a state of prostration after it all! I needed rest and solitude so badly! Was I to stay in Paris? Was I to continue my expeditions with you? No, no, no! I had had enough adventures! Other people's are very interesting, I admit. But when one is one's self the victim and barely escapes with one's life? . . . Oh, my dear friend, how horrible it was! Shall I ever forget it? . . .

"Here, at la Roncière, I enjoy the greatest peace. My old spinster cousin Ermelin pets and coddles me like an invalid. I am getting back my colour and am very well, physically. . . so much so, in fact, that I no longer ever think of interesting myself in other people's business. Never again! For instance (I am only telling you this because you are incorrigible, as inquisitive as any old charwoman, and always ready to busy yourself with things that don't concern you), yesterday I was present at a rather curious meeting. Antoinette had taken me to the inn at Bassicourt, where we were having tea in the public room, among the peasants (it was market-day), when the arrival of three people, two men and a woman, caused a sudden pause in the conversation.

"One of the men was a fat farmer in a long blouse, with a jovial, red face, framed in white whiskers. The other was younger, was dressed in corduroy and had lean, yellow, cross-grained features. Each of them carried a gun slung over his shoulder. Between them was a short, slender young woman, in a brown cloak and a fur cap, whose rather thin and extremely pale face was surprisingly delicate and distinguished-looking.

"'Father, son and daughter-in-law,' whispered my cousin.

"'What! Can that charming creature be the wife of that clod-hopper?'

"'And the daughter-in-law of Baron de Gorne.'

"'Is the old fellow over there a baron?'

"'Yes, descended from a very ancient, noble family which used to own the château in the old days. He has always lived like a peasant: a great hunter, a great drinker, a great litigant, always at law with somebody, now very nearly ruined. His son Mathias was more ambitious and less attached to the soil and studied for the bar. Then he went to America. Next, the lack of money brought him back to the village, whereupon he fell in love with a young girl in the nearest town. The poor girl consented, no one knows why, to marry him; and for five years past she has been leading the life of a hermit, or rather of a prisoner, in a little manor-house close by, the Manoir-au-Puits, the Well Manor.'

"'With the father and the son?' I asked.

"'No, the father lives at the far end of the village, on a lonely farm.'

"'And is Master Mathias jealous?'

"'A perfect tiger!'

"'Without reason?'

"'Without reason, for Natalie de Gorne is the straightest woman in the world and it is not her fault if a handsome young man has been hanging around the manor-house for the past few months. However, the de Gornes can't get over it.'

"'What, the father neither?'

"'The handsome young man is the last descendant of the people who bought the château long ago. This explains old de

Gorne's hatred. Jérôme Vignal—I know him and am very fond of him—is a good-looking fellow and very well off; and he has sworn to run off with Natalie de Gorne. It's the old man who says so, whenever he has had a drop too much. There, listen!'

"The old chap was sitting among a group of men who were amusing themselves by making him drink and plying him with questions. He was already a little bit 'on' and was holding forth with a tone of indignation and a mocking smile which formed the most comic contrast:

"'He's wasting his time, I tell you, the coxcomb! It's no manner of use his poaching round our way and making sheep's-eyes at the wench. . . The coverts are watched! If he comes too near, it means a bullet, eh, Mathias?'

"He gripped his daughter-in-law's hand:

"'And then the little wench knows how to defend herself too,' he chuckled. 'Eh, you don't want any admirers, do you Natalie?'

"The young wife blushed, in her confusion at being addressed in these terms, while her husband growled:

"'You'd do better to hold your tongue, father. There are things one doesn't talk about in public.'

"'Things that affect one's honour are best settled in public,' retorted the old one. 'Where I'm concerned, the honour of the de Gornes comes before everything; and that fine spark, with his Paris airs, sha'n't. . .'

"He stopped short. Before him stood a man who had just come in and who seemed to be waiting for him to finish his sentence. The newcomer was a tall, powerfully-built young fellow, in riding-kit, with a hunting-crop in his hand. His strong and rather stern face was lighted up by a pair of fine eyes in which shone an ironical smile.

"'Jérôme Vignal,' whispered my cousin.

"The young man seemed not at all embarrassed. On seeing Natalie, he made a low bow; and, when Mathias de Gorne took a step forward, he eyed him from head to foot, as though to say:

"'Well, what about it?'

"And his attitude was so haughty and contemptuous that the de Gornes unslung their guns and took them in both hands, like sportsmen about to shoot. The son's expression was very fierce.

"Jérôme was quite unmoved by the threat. After a few seconds, turning to the inn-keeper, he remarked:

"'Oh, I say! I came to see old Vasseur. But his shop is shut. Would you mind giving him the holster of my revolver? It wants a stitch or two.'

"He handed the holster to the inn-keeper and added, laughing:

"'I'm keeping the revolver, in case I need it. You never can tell!'

"Then, still very calmly, he took a cigarette from a silver case, lit it and walked out. We saw him through the window vaulting on his horse and riding off at a slow trot.

"Old de Gorne tossed off a glass of brandy, swearing most horribly.

"His son clapped his hand to the old man's mouth and forced him to sit down. Natalie de Gorne was weeping beside them. . .

"That's my story, dear friend. As you see, it's not tremendously interesting and does not deserve your attention. There's no mystery in it and no part for you to play. Indeed, I particularly insist that you should not seek a pretext for any untimely interference. Of course, I should be glad to see the poor thing protected: she appears to be a perfect martyr. But, as I said before, let us leave other people to get out of their own troubles and go no farther with our little experiments. . ."

RÉNINE FINISHED READING THE LETTER, read it over again and ended by saying:

"That's it. Everything's right as right can be. She doesn't want to continue our little experiments, because this would make the seventh and because she's afraid of the eighth, which under the terms of our agreement has a very particular significance. She doesn't want to. . . and she does want to. . . without seeming to want to."

HE RUBBED HIS HANDS. THE letter was an invaluable witness to the influence which he had gradually, gently and patiently gained over Hortense Daniel. It betrayed a rather complex feeling, composed of admiration, unbounded confidence, uneasiness at times, fear and almost terror, but also love: he was convinced of that. His companion in adventures which she shared with a good fellowship that excluded any awkwardness between them, she had suddenly taken fright; and a sort of modesty, mingled with a certain coquetry; was impelling her to hold back.

That very evening, Sunday, Rénine took the train.

And, at break of day, after covering by diligence, on a road white with snow, the five miles between the little town of Pompignat, where he alighted, and the village of Bassicourt, he learnt that his journey might prove of some use: three shots had been heard during the night in the direction of the Manoir-au-Puits.

"Three shots, sergeant. I heard them as plainly as I see you standing before me," said a peasant whom the gendarmes were questioning in the parlour of the inn which Rénine had entered.

"So did I," said the waiter. "Three shots. It may have been twelve o'clock at night. The snow, which had been falling since nine, had stopped. . . and the shots sounded across the fields, one after the other: bang, bang, bang."

Five more peasants gave their evidence. The sergeant and his men had heard nothing, because the police-station backed on the fields. But a farm-labourer and a woman arrived, who said that they were in Mathias de Gorne's service, that they had been away for two days because of the intervening Sunday and that they had come straight from the manor-house, where they were unable to obtain admission:

"The gate of the grounds is locked, sergeant," said the man. "It's the first time I've known this to happen. M. Mathias comes out to open it himself, every morning at the stroke of six, winter and summer. Well, it's past eight now. I called and shouted. Nobody answered. So we came on here."

"You might have enquired at old M. de Gorne's," said the sergeant. "He lives on the high-road."

"On my word, so I might! I never thought of that."

"We'd better go there now," the sergeant decided. Two of his men went with him, as well as the peasants and a locksmith whose services were called into requisition. Rénine joined the party.

Soon, at the end of the village, they reached old de Gorne's farmyard, which Rénine recognized by Hortense's description of its position.

The old fellow was harnessing his horse and trap. When they told him what had happened, he burst out laughing:

"Three shots? Bang, bang, bang? Why, my dear sergeant, there are only two barrels to Mathias' gun!"

"What about the locked gate?"

"It means that the lad's asleep, that's all. Last night, he came and cracked a bottle with me. . . perhaps two. . . or even three; and he'll be sleeping it off, I expect. . . he and Natalie."

He climbed on to the box of his trap—an old cart with a patched tilt—and cracked his whip:

"Good-bye, gentlemen all. Those three shots of yours won't stop me from going to market at Pompignat, as I do every Monday. I've a couple of calves under the tilt; and they're just fit for the butcher. Good-day to you!"

The others walked on. Rénine went up to the sergeant and gave him his name:

"I'm a friend of Mlle. Ermelin, of La Roncière; and, as it's too early to call on her yet, I shall be glad if you'll allow me to go round by the manor with you. Mlle. Ermelin knows Madame de Gorne; and it will be a satisfaction to me to relieve her mind, for there's nothing wrong at the manor-house, I hope?"

"If there is," replied the sergeant, "we shall read all about it as plainly as on a map, because of the snow."

He was a likable young man and seemed smart and intelligent. From the very first he had shown great acuteness in observing the tracks which Mathias had left behind him, the evening before, on returning home, tracks which soon became confused with the footprints made in going and coming by the farm-labourer and the woman. Meanwhile they came to the walls of a property of which the locksmith readily opened the gate.

From here onward, a single trail appeared upon the spotless snow, that of Mathias; and it was easy to perceive that the son must have shared largely in the father's libations, as the line of footprints described sudden curves which made it swerve right up to the trees of the avenue.

Two hundred yards farther stood the dilapidated two-storeyed building of the Manoir-au-Puits. The principal door was open.

"Let's go in," said the sergeant.

And, the moment he had crossed the threshold, he muttered:

"Oho! Old de Gorne made a mistake in not coming. They've been fighting in here."

The big room was in disorder. Two shattered chairs, the overturned table and much broken glass and china bore witness to the violence

MAURICE LEBLANC

of the struggle. The tall clock, lying on the ground, had stopped at twenty past eleven.

With the farm-girl showing them the way, they ran up to the first floor. Neither Mathias nor his wife was there. But the door of their bedroom had been broken down with a hammer which they discovered under the bed.

Rénine and the sergeant went downstairs again. The living-room had a passage communicating with the kitchen, which lay at the back of the house and opened on a small yard fenced off from the orchard. At the end of this enclosure was a well near which one was bound to pass.

Now, from the door of the kitchen to the well, the snow, which was not very thick, had been pressed down to this side and that, as though a body had been dragged over it. And all around the well were tangled traces of trampling feet, showing that the struggle must have been resumed at this spot. The sergeant again discovered Mathias' footprints, together with others which were shapelier and lighter.

These latter went straight into the orchard, by themselves. And, thirty yards on, near the footprints, a revolver was picked up and recognized by one of the peasants as resembling that which Jérôme Vignal had produced in the inn two days before.

The sergeant examined the cylinder. Three of the seven bullets had been fired.

And so the tragedy was little by little reconstructed in its main outlines; and the sergeant, who had ordered everybody to stand aside and not to step on the site of the footprints, came back to the well, leant over, put a few questions to the farm-girl and, going up to Rénine, whispered:

"It all seems fairly clear to me."

Rénine took his arm:

"Let's speak out plainly, sergeant. I understand the business pretty well, for, as I told you, I know Mlle. Ermelin, who is a friend of Jérôme Vignal's and also knows Madame de Gorne. Do you suppose. . . ?"

"I don't want to suppose anything. I simply declare that some one came there last night. . ."

"By which way? The only tracks of a person coming towards the manor are those of M. de Gorne."

"That's because the other person arrived before the snowfall, that is to say, before nine o'clock."

"Then he must have hidden in a corner of the living-room and waited for the return of M. de Gorne, who came after the snow?"

"Just so. As soon as Mathias came in, the man went for him. There was a fight. Mathias made his escape through the kitchen. The man ran after him to the well and fired three revolver-shots."

"And where's the body?"

"Down the well."

Rénine protested:

"Oh, I say! Aren't you taking a lot for granted?"

"Why, sir, the snow's there, to tell the story; and the snow plainly says that, after the struggle, after the three shots, one man alone walked away and left the farm, one man only, and his footprints are not those of Mathias de Gorne. Then where can Mathias de Gorne be?"

"But the well. . . can be dragged?"

"No. The well is practically bottomless. It is known all over the district and gives its name to the manor."

"So you really believe. . . ?"

"I repeat what I said. Before the snowfall, a single arrival, Mathias, and a single departure, the stranger."

"And Madame de Gorne? Was she too killed and thrown down the well like her husband?"

"No, carried off."

"Carried off?"

"Remember that her bedroom was broken down with a hammer."

"Come, come, sergeant! You yourself declare that there was only one departure, the stranger's."

"Stoop down. Look at the man's footprints. See how they sink into the snow, until they actually touch the ground. Those are the footprints of a man, laden with a heavy burden. The stranger was carrying Madame de Gorne on his shoulder."

"Then there's an outlet this way?"

"Yes, a little door of which Mathias de Gorne always had the key on him. The man must have taken it from him."

"A way out into the open fields?"

"Yes, a road which joins the departmental highway three quarters of a mile from here. . . And do you know where?"

"Where?"

"At the corner of the château."

"Jérôme Vignal's château?"

"By Jove, this is beginning to look serious! If the trail leads to the château and stops there, we shall know where we stand."

The trail did continue to the château, as they were able to perceive after following it across the undulating fields, on which the snow lay heaped in places. The approach to the main gates had been swept, but they saw that another trail, formed by the two wheels of a vehicle, was running in the opposite direction to the village.

The sergeant rang the bell. The porter, who had also been sweeping the drive, came to the gates, with a broom in his hand. In answer to a question, the man said that M. Vignal had gone away that morning before anyone else was up and that he himself had harnessed the horse to the trap.

"In that case," said Rénine, when they had moved away, "all we have to do is to follow the tracks of the wheels."

"That will be no use," said the sergeant. "They have taken the railway."

"At Pompignat station, where I came from? But they would have passed through the village."

"They have gone just the other way, because it leads to the town, where the express trains stop. The procurator-general has an office in the town. I'll telephone; and, as there's no train before eleven o'clock, all that they need do is to keep a watch at the station."

"I think you're doing the right thing, sergeant," said Rénine, "and I congratulate you on the way in which you have carried out your investigation."

They parted. Rénine went back to the inn in the village and sent a note to Hortense Daniel by hand:

My Very Dear Friend,

"I seemed to gather from your letter that, touched as always by anything that concerns the heart, you were anxious to protect the love-affair of Jérôme and Natalie. Now there is every reason to suppose that these two, without consulting their fair protectress, have run away, after throwing Mathias de Gorne down a well.

"Forgive me for not coming to see you. The whole thing is extremely obscure; and, if I were with you, I should not have the detachment of mind which is needed to think the case over."

It was then half-past ten. Rénine went for a walk into the country, with his hands clasped behind his back and without vouchsafing a glance at the exquisite spectacle of the white meadows. He came back for lunch, still absorbed in his thoughts and indifferent to the talk of the customers of the inn, who on all sides were discussing recent events.

He went up to his room and had been asleep some time when he was awakened by a tapping at the door. He got up and opened it:

"Is it you? . . . Is it you?" he whispered.

Hortense and he stood gazing at each other for some seconds in silence, holding each other's hands, as though nothing, no irrelevant thought and no utterance, must be allowed to interfere with the joy of their meeting. Then he asked:

"Was I right in coming?"

"Yes," she said, gently, "I expected you."

"Perhaps it would have been better if you had sent for me sooner, instead of waiting. . . Events did not wait, you see, and I don't quite know what's to become of Jérôme Vignal and Natalie de Gorne."

"What, haven't you heard?" she said, quickly. "They've been arrested. They were going to travel by the express."

"Arrested? No." Rénine objected. "People are not arrested like that. They have to be questioned first."

"That's what's being done now. The authorities are making a search."

"Where?"

"At the château. And, as they are innocent. . . For they are innocent, aren't they? You don't admit that they are guilty, any more than I do?"

He replied:

"I admit nothing, I can admit nothing, my dear. Nevertheless, I am bound to say that everything is against them. . . except one fact, which is that everything is too much against them. It is not normal for so many proofs to be heaped up one on top of the other and for the man who commits a murder to tell his story so frankly. Apart from this, there's nothing but mystery and discrepancy."

"Well?"

"Well, I am greatly puzzled."

"But you have a plan?"

"None at all, so far. Ah, if I could see him, Jérôme Vignal, and her, Natalie de Gorne, and hear them and know what they are saying in their own defence! But you can understand that I sha'n't be permitted either to ask them any questions or to be present at their examination. Besides, it must be finished by this time."

"It's finished at the château," she said, "but it's going to be continued at the manor-house."

"Are they taking them to the manor-house?" he asked eagerly.

"Yes. . . at least, judging by what was said to the chauffeur of one of the procurator's two cars."

"Oh, in that case," exclaimed Rénine, "the thing's done! The manor-house! Why, we shall be in the front row of the stalls! We shall see and hear everything; and, as a word, a tone of the voice, a quiver of the eyelids will be enough to give me the tiny clue I need, we may entertain some hope. Come along."

He took her by the direct route which he had followed that morning, leading to the gate which the locksmith had opened. The gendarmes on duty at the manor-house had made a passage through the snow, beside the line of footprints and around the house. Chance enabled Rénine and Hortense to approach unseen and through a side-window to enter a corridor near a back-staircase. A few steps up was a little chamber which received its only light through a sort of bull's-eye, from the large room on the ground-floor. Rénine, during the morning visit, had noticed the bull's-eye, which was covered on the inside with a piece of cloth. He removed the cloth and cut out one of the panes.

A few minutes later, a sound of voices rose from the other side of the house, no doubt near the well. The sound grew more distinct. A number of people flocked into the house. Some of them went up stairs to the first floor, while the sergeant arrived with a young man of whom Rénine and Hortense were able to distinguish only the tall figure:

"Jérôme Vignal," said she.

"Yes," said Rénine. "They are examining Madame de Gorne first, upstairs, in her bedroom."

A quarter of an hour passed. Then the persons on the first floor came downstairs and went in. They were the procurator's deputy, his clerk, a commissary of police and two detectives.

Madame de Gorne was shown in and the deputy asked Jérôme Vignal to step forward.

Jérôme Vignal's face was certainly that of the strong man whom Hortense had depicted in her letter. He displayed no uneasiness, but rather decision and a resolute will. Natalie, who was short and very slight, with a feverish light in her eyes, nevertheless produced the same impression of quiet confidence.

The deputy, who was examining the disordered furniture and the traces of the struggle, invited her to sit down and said to Jérôme:

"Monsieur, I have not asked you many questions so far. This is a summary enquiry which I am conducting in your presence and which will be continued later by the examining-magistrate; and I wished above all to explain to you the very serious reasons for which I asked you to interrupt your journey and to come back here with Madame de Gorne. You are now in a position to refute the truly distressing charges that are hanging over you. I therefore ask you to tell me the exact truth."

"Mr. Deputy," replied Jérôme, "the charges in question trouble me very little. The truth for which you are asking will defeat all the lies which chance has accumulated against me. It is this."

He reflected for an instant and then, in clear, frank tones, said:

"I love Madame de Gorne. The first time I met her, I conceived the greatest sympathy and admiration for her. But my affection has always been directed by the sole thought of her happiness. I love her, but I respect her even more. Madame de Gorne must have told you and I tell you again that she and I exchanged our first few words last night."

He continued, in a lower voice:

"I respect her the more inasmuch as she is exceedingly unhappy. All the world knows that every minute of her life was a martyrdom. Her husband persecuted her with ferocious hatred and frantic jealousy. Ask the servants. They will tell you of the long suffering of Natalie de Gorne, of the blows which she received and the insults which she had to endure. I tried to stop this torture by restoring to the rights of appeal which the merest stranger may claim when unhappiness and injustice pass a certain limit. I went three times to old de Gorne and begged him to interfere; but I found in him an almost equal hatred towards his daughter-in-law, the hatred which many people feel for anything beautiful and noble. At last I resolved on direct action and last night I took a step with regard to Mathias de Gorne which was. . . a little unusual, I admit, but which seemed likely to succeed, considering the man's character. I swear, Mr. Deputy, that I had no other intention than to talk to Mathias de Gorne. Knowing certain particulars of his life which enabled me to bring effective pressure to bear upon him, I wished to make use of this advantage in order to achieve my purpose. If things turned out differently, I am not wholly to blame. . . So I went there a little before nine o'clock. The servants, I knew, were out. He opened the door himself. He was alone."

"Monsieur," said the deputy, interrupting him, "you are saying something—as Madame de Gorne, for that matter, did just now—which is manifestly opposed to the truth. Mathias de Gorne did not come home last night until eleven o'clock. We have two definite proofs of this: his father's evidence and the prints of his feet in the snow, which fell from a quarter past nine o'clock to eleven."

"Mr. Deputy," Jérôme Vignal declared, without heeding the bad effect which his obstinacy was producing, "I am relating things as they were and not as they may be interpreted. But to continue. That clock marked ten minutes to nine when I entered this room. M. de Gorne, believing that he was about to be attacked, had taken down his gun. I placed my revolver on the table, out of reach of my hand, and sat down: 'I want to speak to you, monsieur,' I said. 'Please listen to me.' He did not stir and did not utter a single syllable. So I spoke. And straightway, crudely, without any previous explanations which might have softened the bluntness of my proposal, I spoke the few words which I had prepared beforehand: 'I have spent some months, monsieur,' I said, 'in making careful enquiries into your financial position. You have mortgaged every foot of your land. You have signed bills which will shortly be falling due and which it will be absolutely impossible for you to honour. You have nothing to hope for from your father, whose own affairs are in a very bad condition. So you are ruined. I have come to save you.' . . . He watched me, still without speaking, and sat down, which I took to mean that my suggestion was not entirely displeasing. Then I took a sheaf of bank-notes from my pocket, placed it before him and continued: 'Here is sixty thousand francs, monsieur. I will buy the Manoir-au-Puits, its lands and dependencies and take over the mortgages. The sum named is exactly twice what they are worth.' . . . I saw his eyes glittering. He asked my conditions. 'Only one,' I said, 'that you go to America.' . . . Mr. Deputy, we sat discussing for two hours. It was not that my offer roused his indignation—I should not have risked it if I had not known with whom I was dealing—but he wanted more and haggled greedily, though he refrained from mentioning the name of Madame de Gorne, to whom I myself had not once alluded. We might have been two men engaged in a dispute and seeking an agreement on common ground, whereas it was the happiness and the whole destiny of a woman that were at stake. At last, weary of the discussion, I accepted a compromise and we came to terms, which I resolved to make definite then and there. Two letters were exchanged between us: one in which he made the Manoir-au-Puits over to me for the sum which I had paid him; and one, which he pocketed immediately, by which I was to send him as much more in America on the day on which the decree of divorce was pronounced. . . So the affair was settled. I am sure that at that moment he was accepting in good faith. He looked upon me less as an enemy and a rival than as a man who was doing him a service. He even went so far as to give me the key of the little door which opens on the fields, so that I might go home by the short cut. Unfortunately, while I was picking up my cap and greatcoat, I made the mistake of leaving on the table the letter of sale which he had signed. In a moment, Mathias de Gorne had seen the advantage which he could take of my slip: he could keep his property, keep his wife. . . and keep the money. Quick as lightning, he tucked away the paper, hit me over the head with the butt-end of his gun, threw the gun on the floor and seized me by the throat with both hands. He had reckoned without his host. I was the stronger of the two; and after a sharp but short struggle, I mastered him and tied him up with a cord which I found lying in a corner. . . Mr. Deputy, if my enemy's resolve was sudden, mine was no less so. Since, when all was said, he had accepted the bargain, I would force him to keep it, at least in so far as I was interested. A very few steps brought me to the first floor. . . I had not a doubt that Madame de Gorne was there and had heard the sound of our discussion. Switching on the light of my pocket-torch, I looked into three bedrooms. The fourth was locked. I knocked at the door. There was no reply. But this was one of the moments in which a man allows no obstacle to stand in his way. I had seen a hammer in one of the rooms. I picked it up and smashed in the door. . . Yes, Natalie was lying there, on the floor, in a dead faint. I took her in my arms, carried her downstairs and went through the kitchen. On seeing the snow outside, I at once realized that my footprints would be easily traced. But what did it matter? Was there any reason why I should put Mathias de Gorne off the scent? Not at all. With the sixty thousand francs in his possession, as well as the paper in which I undertook to pay him a like sum on the day of his divorce, to say nothing of his house and land, he would go away, leaving Natalie de Gorne to me. Nothing was changed between us, except one thing: instead of awaiting his good pleasure, I had at once seized the precious pledge which I coveted. What I feared, therefore, was not so much any subsequent attack on the part of Mathias de Gorne, but rather the indignant reproaches of his wife. What would she say when she realized that she was a prisoner in my hands? . . . The reasons why I escaped reproach Madame de Gorne has, I believe, had the frankness to tell you. Love calls forth love. That night, in my house, broken by emotion, she confessed her feeling for me. She loved me as I loved her. Our destinies were henceforth mingled. She and I set out at five o'clock this morning. . . not foreseeing for an instant that we were amenable to the law."

Jérôme Vignal's story was finished. He had told it straight off the reel, like a story learnt by heart and incapable of revision in any detail.

There was a brief pause, during which Hortense whispered:

"It all sounds quite possible and, in any case, very logical."

"There are the objections to come," said Rénine. "Wait till you hear them. They are very serious. There's one in particular. . ."

The deputy-procurator stated it at once:

"And what became of M. de Gorne in all this?"

"Mathias de Gorne?" asked Jérôme.

"Yes. You have related, with an accent of great sincerity, a series of facts which I am quite willing to admit. Unfortunately, you have forgotten a point of the first importance: what became of Mathias de Gorne? You tied him up here, in this room. Well, this morning he was gone."

"Of course, Mr. Deputy, Mathias de Gorne accepted the bargain in the end and went away."

"By what road?"

"No doubt by the road that leads to his father's house."

"Where are his footprints? The expanse of snow is an impartial witness. After your fight with him, we see you, on the snow, moving away. Why don't we see him? He came and did not go away again. Where is he? There is not a trace of him. . . or rather. . ."

The deputy lowered his voice:

"Or rather, yes, there are some traces on the way to the well and around the well. . . traces which prove that the last struggle of all took place there. . . And after that there is nothing. . . not a thing. . ."

Jérôme shrugged his shoulders:

"You have already mentioned this, Mr. Deputy, and it implies a charge of homicide against me. I have nothing to say to it."

"Have you anything to say to the fact that your revolver was picked up within fifteen yards of the well?"

"No."

"Or to the strange coincidence between the three shots heard in the night and the three cartridges missing from your revolver?"

"No, Mr. Deputy, there was not, as you believe, a last struggle by the well, because I left M. de Gorne tied up, in this room, and because I also left my revolver here. On the other hand, if shots were heard, they were not fired by me."

"A casual coincidence, therefore?"

"That's a matter for the police to explain. My only duty is to tell the truth and you are not entitled to ask more of me."

"And if that truth conflicts with the facts observed?"

"It means that the facts are wrong, Mr. Deputy."

"As you please. But, until the day when the police are able to make them agree with your statements, you will understand that I am obliged to keep you under arrest."

"And Madame de Gorne?" asked Jérôme, greatly distressed.

The deputy did not reply. He exchanged a few words with the commissary of police and then, beckoning to a detective, ordered him to bring up one of the two motor-cars. Then he turned to Natalie:

"Madame, you have heard M. Vignal's evidence. It agrees word for word with your own. M. Vignal declares in particular that you had fainted when he carried you away. But did you remain unconscious all the way?"

It seemed as though Jérôme's composure had increased Madame de Gorne's assurance. She replied:

"I did not come to, monsieur, until I was at the château."

"It's most extraordinary. Didn't you hear the three shots which were heard by almost every one in the village?"

"I did not."

"And did you see nothing of what happened beside the well?"

"Nothing did happen. M. Vignal has told you so."

"Then what has become of your husband?"

"I don't know."

"Come, madame, you really must assist the officers of the law and at least tell us what you think. Do you believe that there may have been an accident and that possibly M. de Gorne, who had been to see his father and had more to drink than usual, lost his balance and fell into the well?"

"When my husband came back from seeing his father, he was not in the least intoxicated."

"His father, however, has stated that he was. His father and he had drunk two or three bottles of wine."

"His father is not telling the truth."

"But the snow tells the truth, madame," said the deputy, irritably. "And the line of his footprints wavers from side to side."

"My husband came in at half-past-eight, monsieur, before the snow had begun to fall."

The deputy struck the table with his fist:

"But, really, madame, you're going right against the evidence! . . . That sheet of snow cannot speak false! . . . I may accept your denial of matters that cannot be verified. But these footprints in the snow. . . in the snow. . ."

He controlled himself.

The motor-car drew up outside the windows. Forming a sudden resolve, he said to Natalie:

"You will be good enough to hold yourself at the disposal of the authorities, madame, and to remain here, in the manor-house. . ."

And he made a sign to the sergeant to remove Jérôme Vignal in the car.

The game was lost for the two lovers. Barely united, they had to separate and to fight, far away from each other, against the most grievous accusations.

Jérôme took a step towards Natalie. They exchanged a long, sorrowful look. Then he bowed to her and walked to the door, in the wake of the sergeant of gendarmes.

"Halt!" cried a voice. "Sergeant, right about. . . turn! . . . Jérôme Vignal, stay where you are!"

The ruffled deputy raised his head, as did the other people present. The voice came from the ceiling. The bulls-eye window had opened and Rénine, leaning through it, was waving his arms:

"I wish to be heard! . . . I have several remarks to make. . . especially in respect of the zigzag footprints! . . . It all lies in that! . . . Mathias had not been drinking! . . ."

He had turned round and put his two legs through the opening, saying to Hortense, who tried to prevent him:

"Don't move. . . No one will disturb you."

And, releasing his hold, he dropped into the room.

The deputy appeared dumfounded:

"But, really, monsieur, who are you? Where do you come from?"

Rénine brushed the dust from his clothes and replied:

"Excuse me, Mr. Deputy. I ought to have come the same way as everybody else. But I was in a hurry. Besides, if I had come in by the door instead of falling from the ceiling, my words would not have made the same impression."

The infuriated deputy advanced to meet him:

"Who are you?"

"Prince Rénine. I was with the sergeant this morning when he was pursuing his investigations, wasn't I, sergeant? Since then I have been hunting about for information. That's why, wishing to be present at the hearing, I found a corner in a little private room. . ."

"You were there? You had the audacity? . . ."

"One must needs be audacious, when the truth's at stake. If I had not been there, I should not have discovered just the one little clue which I missed. I should not have known that Mathias de Gorne was not the least bit drunk. Now that's the key to the riddle. When we know that, we know the solution."

The deputy found himself in a rather ridiculous position. Since he had failed to take the necessary precautions to ensure the secrecy of his enquiry, it was difficult for him to take any steps against this interloper. He growled:

"Let's have done with this. What are you asking?"

"A few minutes of your kind attention."

"And with what object?"

"To establish the innocence of M. Vignal and Madame de Gorne."

He was wearing that calm air, that sort of indifferent look which was peculiar to him in moments of actions when the crisis of the drama depended solely upon himself. Hortense felt a thrill pass through her and at once became full of confidence:

"They're saved," she thought, with sudden emotion. "I asked him to protect that young creature; and he is saving her from prison and despair."

Jérôme and Natalie must have experienced the same impression of sudden hope, for they had drawn nearer to each other, as though this stranger, descended from the clouds, had already given them the right to clasp hands.

The deputy shrugged his shoulders:

"The prosecution will have every means, when the time comes, of establishing their innocence for itself. You will be called."

MAURICE LEBLANC

"It would be better to establish it here and now. Any delay might lead to grievous consequences."

"I happen to be in a hurry."

"Two or three minutes will do."

"Two or three minutes to explain a case like this!"

"No longer, I assure you."

"Are you as certain of it as all that?"

"I am now. I have been thinking hard since this morning."

The deputy realized that this was one of those gentry who stick to you like a leech and that there was nothing for it but to submit. In a rather bantering tone, he asked:

"Does your thinking enable you to tell us the exact spot where M. Mathias de Gorne is at this moment?"

Rénine took out his watch and answered:

"In Paris, Mr. Deputy."

"In Paris? Alive then?"

"Alive and, what is more, in the pink of health."

"I am delighted to hear it. But then what's the meaning of the footprints around the well and the presence of that revolver and those three shots?"

"Simply camouflage."

"Oh, really? Camouflage contrived by whom?"

"By Mathias de Gorne himself."

"That's curious! And with what object?"

"With the object of passing himself off for dead and of arranging subsequent matters in such a way that M. Vignal was bound to be accused of the death, the murder."

"An ingenious theory," the deputy agreed, still in a satirical tone. "What do you think of it, M. Vignal?"

"It is a theory which flashed through my own mind. Mr. Deputy," replied Jérôme. "It is quite likely that, after our struggle and after I had gone, Mathias de Gorne conceived a new plan by which, this time, his hatred would be fully gratified. He both loved and detested his wife. He held me in the greatest loathing. This must be his revenge."

"His revenge would cost him dear, considering that, according to your statement, Mathias de Gorne was to receive a second sum of sixty thousand francs from you."

"He would receive that sum in another quarter, Mr. Deputy. My examination of the financial position of the de Gorne family revealed to me the fact that the father and son had taken out a life-insurance policy in each other's favour. With the son dead, or passing for dead, the father would receive the insurance-money and indemnify his son."

"You mean to say," asked the deputy, with a smile, "that in all this camouflage, as you call it, M. de Gorne the elder would act as his son's accomplice?"

Rénine took up the challenge:

"Just so, Mr. Deputy. The father and son are accomplices.

"Then we shall find the son at the father's?"

"You would have found him there last night."

"What became of him?"

"He took the train at Pompignat."

"That's a mere supposition."

"No, a certainty."

"A moral certainty, perhaps, but you'll admit there's not the slightest proof."

The deputy did not wait for a reply. He considered that he had displayed an excessive goodwill and that patience has its limits and he put an end to the interview:

"Not the slightest proof," he repeated, taking up his hat. "And, above all, . . . above all, there's nothing in what you've said that can contradict in the very least the evidence of that relentless witness, the snow. To go to his father, Mathias de Gorne must have left this house. Which way did he go?"

"Hang it all, M. Vignal told you: by the road which leads from here to his father's!"

"There are no tracks in the snow."

"Yes, there are."

"But they show him coming here and not going away from here."

"It's the same thing."

"What?"

"Of course it is. There's more than one way of walking. One doesn't always go ahead by following one's nose."

"In what other way can one go ahead?"

"By walking backwards, Mr. Deputy."

These few words, spoken very simply, but in a clear tone which gave full value to every syllable, produced a profound silence. Those present at once grasped their extreme significance and, by adapting it to the actual happenings, perceived in a flash the impenetrable truth, which suddenly appeared to be the most natural thing in the world.

Rénine continued his argument. Stepping backwards in the direction of the window, he said:

"If I want to get to that window, I can of course walk straight up to it; but I can just as easily turn my back to it and walk that way. In either case I reach my goal."

And he at once proceeded in a vigorous tone:

"Here's the gist of it all. At half-past eight, before the snow fell, M. de Gorne comes home from his father's house. M. Vignal arrives twenty minutes later. There is a long discussion and a struggle, taking up three hours in all. It is then, after M. Vignal has carried off Madame de Gorne and made his escape, that Mathias de Gorne, foaming at the mouth, wild with rage, but suddenly seeing his chance of taking the most terrible revenge, hits upon the ingenious idea of using against his enemy the very snowfall upon whose evidence you are now relying. He therefore plans his own murder, or rather the appearance of his murder and of his fall to the bottom of the well and makes off backwards, step by step, thus recording his arrival instead of his departure on the white page."

The deputy sneered no longer. This eccentric intruder suddenly appeared to him in the light of a person worthy of attention, whom it would not do to make fun of. He asked:

"And how could he have left his father's house?"

"In a trap, quite simply."

"Who drove it?"

"The father. This morning the sergeant and I saw the trap and spoke to the father, who was going to market as usual. The son was hidden under the tilt. He took the train at Pompignat and is in Paris by now."

Rénine's explanation, as promised, had taken hardly five minutes. He had based it solely on logic and the probabilities of the case. And yet not a jot was left of the distressing mystery in which they were floundering. The darkness was dispelled. The whole truth appeared.

Madame de Gorne wept for joy and Jérôme Vignal thanked the good genius who was changing the course of events with a stroke of his magic wand.

"Shall we examine those footprints together, Mr. Deputy?" asked Rénine. "Do you mind? The mistake which the sergeant and I made this morning was to investigate only the footprints left by the alleged murderer and to neglect Mathias de Gorne's. Why indeed should they have attracted our attention? Yet it was precisely there that the crux of the whole affair was to be found."

They stepped into the orchard and went to the well. It did not need a long examination to observe that many of the footprints were awkward, hesitating, too deeply sunk at the heel and toe and differing from one another in the angle at which the feet were turned.

"This clumsiness was unavoidable," said Rénine. "Mathias de Gorne would have needed a regular apprenticeship before his backward progress could have equalled his ordinary gait; and both his father and he must have been aware of this, at least as regards the zigzags which you see here since old de Gorne went out of his way to tell the sergeant that his son had had too much drink." And he added "Indeed it was the detection of this falsehood that suddenly enlightened me. When Madame de Gorne stated that her husband was not drunk, I thought of the footprints and guessed the truth."

The deputy frankly accepted his part in the matter and began to laugh:

"There's nothing left for it but to send detectives after the bogus corpse."

"On what grounds, Mr. Deputy?" asked Rénine. "Mathias de Gorne has committed no offence against the law. There's nothing criminal in trampling the soil around a well, in shifting the position of a revolver that doesn't belong to you, in firing three shots or in walking backwards to one's father's house. What can we ask of him? The sixty thousand francs? I presume that this is not M. Vignal's intention and that he does not mean to bring a charge against him?"

"Certainly not," said Jérôme.

"Well, what then? The insurance-policy in favour of the survivor? But there would be no misdemeanour unless the father claimed payment. And I should be greatly surprised if he did. . . Hullo, here the old chap is! You'll soon know all about it."

Old de Gorne was coming along, gesticulating as he walked. His easy-going features were screwed up to express sorrow and anger.

"Where's my son?" he cried. "It seems the brute's killed him! . . . My poor Mathias dead! Oh, that scoundrel of a Vignal!"

And he shook his fist at Jérôme.

The deputy said, bluntly:

"A word with you, M. de Gorne. Do you intend to claim your rights under a certain insurance-policy?"

"Well, what do *you* think?" said the old man, off his guard.

"The fact is. . . your son's not dead. People are even saying that you were a partner in his little schemes and that you stuffed him under the tilt of your trap and drove him to the station."

The old fellow spat on the ground, stretched out his hand as though he were going to take a solemn oath, stood for an instant without moving and then, suddenly, changing his mind and his tactics with ingenuous cynicism, he relaxed his features, assumed a conciliatory attitude and burst out laughing:

"That blackguard Mathias! So he tried to pass himself off as dead? What a rascal! And he reckoned on me to collect the insurance-money and send it to him? As if I should be capable of such a low, dirty trick! . . . You don't know me, my boy!"

And, without waiting for more, shaking with merriment like a jolly old fellow amused by a funny story, he took his departure, not forgetting, however, to set his great hob-nail boots on each of the compromising footprints which his son had left behind him.

LATER, WHEN RÉNINE WENT BACK to the manor to let Hortense out, he found that she had disappeared.

He called and asked for her at her cousin Ermelin's. Hortense sent down word asking him to excuse her: she was feeling a little tired and was lying down.

"Capital!" thought Rénine. "Capital! She avoids me, therefore she loves me. The end is not far off."

VIII

At the Sign of Mercury

To Madame Daniel,
La Roncière,
near Bassicourt.

My Dearest Friend,—

"There has been no letter from you for a fortnight; so I
don't expect now to receive one for that troublesome date
of the 5th of December, which we fixed as the last day of
our partnership. I rather wish it would come, because you
will then be released from a contract which no longer seems
to give you pleasure. To me the seven battles which we
fought and won together were a time of endless delight and
enthusiasm. I was living beside you. I was conscious of all the
good which that more active and stirring existence was doing
you. My happiness was so great that I dared not speak of it
to you or let you see anything of my secret feelings except my
desire to please you and my passionate devotion. To-day you
have had enough of your brother in arms. Your will shall be
law.

"But, though I bow to your decree, may I remind you
what it was that I always believed our final adventure would
be? May I repeat your words, not one of which I have
forgotten?

"'I demand,' you said, 'that you shall restore to me a small,
antique clasp, made of a cornelian set in a filigree mount. It
came to me from my mother; and every one knew that it
used to bring her happiness and me too. Since the day when
it vanished from my jewel-case, I have had nothing but
unhappiness. Restore it to me, my good genius.'

"And, when I asked you when the clasp had disappeared,
you answered, with a laugh:

"'Seven years ago. . . or eight. . . or nine: I don't know exactly. . . I don't know when. . . I don't know how. . . I know nothing about it. . .'

"You were challenging me, were you not, and you set me that condition because it was one which I could not fulfil? Nevertheless, I promised and I should like to keep my promise. What I have tried to do, in order to place life before you in a more favourable light, would seem purposeless, if your confidence feels the lack of this talisman to which you attach so great a value. We must not laugh at these little superstitions. They are often the mainspring of our best actions.

"Dear friend, if you had helped me, I should have achieved yet one more victory. Alone and hard pushed by the proximity of the date, I have failed, not however without placing things on such a footing that the undertaking if you care to follow it up, has the greatest chance of success.

"And you will follow it up, won't you? We have entered into a mutual agreement which we are bound to honour. It behooves us, within a fixed time, to inscribe in the book of our common life eight good stories, to which we shall have brought energy, logic, perseverance, some subtlety and occasionally a little heroism. This is the eighth of them. It is for you to act so that it may be written in its proper place on the 5th of December, before the clock strikes eight in the evening.

"And, on that day, you will act as I shall now tell you.

"First of all—and above all, my dear, do not complain that my instructions are fanciful: each of them is an indispensable condition of success—first of all, cut in your cousin's garden three slender lengths of rush. Plait them together and bind up the two ends so as to make a rude switch, like a child's whip-lash.

"When you get to Paris, buy a long necklace of jet beads, cut into facets, and shorten it so that it consists of seventy-five beads, of almost equal size.

"Under your winter cloak, wear a blue woollen gown. On your head, a toque with red leaves on it. Round your neck, a feather boa. No gloves. No rings.

"In the afternoon, take a cab along the left bank of the river to the church of Saint-Étienne-du-Mont. At four o'clock exactly, there will be, near the holy-water basin, just inside the church, an old woman dressed in black, saying her prayers on a silver rosary. She will offer you holy water. Give her your necklace. She will count the beads and hand it back to you. After this, you will walk behind her, you will cross an arm of the Seine and she will lead you, down a lonely street in the Ile Saint-Louis, to a house which you will enter by yourself.

"On the ground-floor of this house, you will find a youngish man with a very pasty complexion. Take off your cloak and then say to him:

"'I have come to fetch my clasp.'

"Do not be astonished by his agitation or dismay. Keep calm in his presence. If he questions you, if he wants to know your reason for applying to him or what impels you to make that request, give him no explanation. Your replies must be confined to these brief formulas:

"'I have come to fetch what belongs to me. I don't know you, I don't know your name; but I am obliged to come to you like this. I must have my clasp returned to me. I must.'

"I honestly believe that, if you have the firmness not to swerve from that attitude, whatever farce the man may play, you will be completely successful. But the contest must be a short one and the issue will depend solely on your confidence in yourself and your certainty of success. It will be a sort of match in which you must defeat your opponent in the first round. If you remain impassive, you will win. If you show hesitation or uneasiness, you can do nothing against him. He will escape you and regain the upper hand after a first moment of distress; and the game will be lost in a few minutes. There is no midway house between victory or. . . defeat.

"In the latter event, you would be obliged—I beg you to pardon me for saying so—again to accept my collaboration. I offer it you in advance, my dear, and without any conditions, while stating quite plainly that all that I have been able to do for you and all that I may yet do gives me no other right than that of thanking you and devoting myself more than ever to the woman who represents my joy, my whole life."

HORTENSE, AFTER READING THE LETTER, folded it up and put it away at the back of a drawer, saying, in a resolute voice:

"I sha'n't go."

To begin with, although she had formerly attached some slight importance to this trinket, which she had regarded as a mascot, she felt very little interest in it now that the period of her trials was apparently at an end. She could not forget that figure eight, which was the serial number of the next adventure. To launch herself upon it meant taking up the interrupted chain, going back to Rénine and giving him a pledge which, with his powers of suggestion, he would know how to turn to account.

Two days before the 5th of December, she was still in the same frame of mind. So she was on the morning of the 4th; but suddenly, without even having to contend against preliminary subterfuges, she ran out into the garden, cut three lengths of rush, plaited them as she used to do in her childhood and at twelve o'clock had herself driven to the station. She was uplifted by an eager curiosity. She was unable to resist all the amusing and novel sensations which the adventure, proposed by Rénine, promised her. It was really too tempting. The jet necklace, the toque with the autumn leaves, the old woman with the silver rosary: how could she resist their mysterious appeal and how could she refuse this opportunity of showing Rénine what she was capable of doing?

"And then, after all," she said to herself, laughing, "he's summoning me to Paris. Now eight o'clock is dangerous to me at a spot three hundred miles from Paris, in that old deserted Château de Halingre, but nowhere else. The only clock that can strike the threatening hour is down there, under lock and key, a prisoner!"

She reached Paris that evening. On the morning of the 5th she went out and bought a jet necklace, which she reduced to seventy-five beads, put on a blue gown and a toque with red leaves and, at four o'clock precisely, entered the church of Saint-Étienne-du-Mont.

Her heart was throbbing violently. This time she was alone; and how acutely she now felt the strength of that support which, from unreflecting fear rather than any reasonable motive, she had thrust aside! She looked around her, almost hoping to see him. But there was no one there. . . no one except an old lady in black, standing beside the holy water basin.

Hortense went up to her. The old lady, who held a silver rosary in her hands, offered her holy water and then began to count the beads of the necklace which Hortense gave her.

She whispered:

"Seventy-five. That's right. Come."

Without another word, she toddled along under the light of the street-lamps, crossed the Pont des Tournelles to the Ile Saint-Louis and went down an empty street leading to a cross-roads, where she stopped in front of an old house with wrought-iron balconies:

"Go in," she said.

And the old lady went away.

Hortense now saw a prosperous-looking shop which occupied almost the whole of the ground-floor and whose windows, blazing with electric light, displayed a huddled array of old furniture and antiquities. She stood there for a few seconds, gazing at it absently. A sign-board bore the words "The Mercury," together with the name of the owner of the shop, "Pancaldi." Higher up, on a projecting cornice which ran on a level with the first floor, a small niche sheltered a terra-cotta Mercury poised on one foot, with wings to his sandals and the caduceus in his hand, who, as Hortense noted, was leaning a little too far forward in the ardour of his flight and ought logically to have lost his balance and taken a header into the street.

"Now!" she said, under her breath.

She turned the handle of the door and walked in.

Despite the ringing of the bells actuated by the opening door, no one came to meet her. The shop seemed to be empty. However, at the extreme end there was a room at the back of the shop and after that another, both crammed with furniture and knick-knacks, many of which looked very valuable. Hortense followed a narrow gangway which twisted and turned between two walls built up of cupboards, cabinets and console-tables, went up two steps and found herself in the last room of all.

A man was sitting at a writing-desk and looking through some account-books. Without turning his head, he said:

"I am at your service, madam. . . Please look round you. . ."

This room contained nothing but articles of a special character which gave it the appearance of some alchemist's laboratory in the middle ages: stuffed owls, skeletons, skulls, copper alembics, astrolabes and all around, hanging on the walls, amulets of every description, mainly hands of ivory or coral with two fingers pointing to ward off ill-luck.

"Are you wanting anything in particular, madam?" asked M. Pancaldi, closing his desk and rising from his chair.

"It's the man," thought Hortense.

He had in fact an uncommonly pasty complexion. A little forked beard, flecked with grey, lengthened his face, which was surmounted by a bald, pallid forehead, beneath which gleamed a pair of small, prominent, restless, shifty eyes.

Hortense, who had not removed her veil or cloak, replied:

"I want a clasp."

"They're in this show-case," he said, leading the way to the connecting room.

Hortense glanced over the glass case and said:

"No, no, . . . I don't see what I'm looking for. I don't want just any clasp, but a clasp which I lost out of a jewel-case some years ago and which I have to look for here."

She was astounded to see the commotion displayed on his features. His eyes became haggard.

"Here? . . . I don't think you are in the least likely. . . What sort of clasp is it? . . ."

"A cornelian, mounted in gold filigree. . . of the 1830 period."

"I don't understand," he stammered. "Why do you come to me?"

She now removed her veil and laid aside her cloak.

He stepped back, as though terrified by the sight of her, and whispered:

"The blue gown! . . . The toque! . . . And—can I believe my eyes?— the jet necklace! . . ."

It was perhaps the whip-lash formed of three rushes that excited him most violently. He pointed his finger at it, began to stagger where he stood and ended by beating the air with his arms, like a drowning man, and fainting away in a chair.

Hortense did not move.

"Whatever farce he may play," Rénine had written, "have the courage to remain impassive."

Perhaps he was not playing a farce. Nevertheless she forced herself to be calm and indifferent.

This lasted for a minute or two, after which M. Pancaldi recovered from his swoon, wiped away the perspiration streaming down his forehead and, striving to control himself, resumed, in a trembling voice:

"Why do you apply to me?"

"Because the clasp is in your possession."

"Who told you that?" he said, without denying the accusation. "How do you know?"

"I know because it is so. Nobody has told me anything. I came here positive that I should find my clasp and with the immovable determination to take it away with me."

"But do you know me? Do you know my name?"

"I don't know you. I did not know your name before I read it over your shop. To me you are simply the man who is going to give me back what belongs to me."

He was greatly agitated. He kept on walking to and fro in a small empty space surrounded by a circle of piled-up furniture, at which he hit out idiotically, at the risk of bringing it down.

Hortense felt that she had the whip hand of him; and, profiting by his confusion, she said, suddenly, in a commanding and threatening tone:

"Where is the thing? You must give it back to me. I insist upon it."

Pancaldi gave way to a moment of despair. He folded his hands and mumbled a few words of entreaty. Then, defeated and suddenly resigned, he said, more distinctly:

"You insist? . . ."

"I do. You must give it to me."

"Yes, yes, I must. . . I agree."

"Speak!" she ordered, more harshly still.

"Speak, no, but write: I will write my secret. . . And that will be the end of me."

He turned to his desk and feverishly wrote a few lines on a sheet of paper, which he put into an envelope and sealed it:

"See," he said, "here's my secret. . . It was my whole life. . ."

And, so saying, he suddenly pressed against his temple a revolver which he had produced from under a pile of papers and fired.

With a quick movement, Hortense struck up his arm. The bullet struck the mirror of a cheval-glass. But Pancaldi collapsed and began to groan, as though he were wounded.

Hortense made a great effort not to lose her composure:

"Rénine warned me," she reflected. "The man's a play-actor. He has kept the envelope. He has kept his revolver, I won't be taken in by him."

Nevertheless, she realized that, despite his apparent calmness, the attempt at suicide and the revolver-shot had completely unnerved her. All her energies were dispersed, like the sticks of a bundle whose string has been cut; and she had a painful impression that the man, who was grovelling at her feet, was in reality slowly getting the better of her.

She sat down, exhausted. As Rénine had foretold, the duel had not lasted longer than a few minutes but it was she who had succumbed, thanks to her feminine nerves and at the very moment when she felt entitled to believe that she had won.

The man Pancaldi was fully aware of this; and, without troubling to invent a transition, he ceased his jeremiads, leapt to his feet, cut a sort of agile caper before Hortense' eyes and cried, in a jeering tone:

"Now we are going to have a little chat; but it would be a nuisance to be at the mercy of the first passing customer, wouldn't it?"

He ran to the street-door, opened it and pulled down the iron shutter which closed the shop. Then, still hopping and skipping, he came back to Hortense:

"Oof! I really thought I was done for! One more effort, madam, and you would have pulled it off. But then I'm such a simple chap! It seemed to me that you had come from the back of beyond, as an emissary of Providence, to call me to account; and, like a fool, I was about to give the thing back. . . Ah, Mlle. Hortense—let me call you so: I used to know you by that name—Mlle. Hortense, what you lack, to use a vulgar expression, is gut."

He sat down beside her and, with a malicious look, said, savagely:

"The time has come to speak out. Who contrived this business? Not you; eh? It's not in your style. Then who? . . . I have always been honest in my life, scrupulously honest. . . except once. . . in the matter of that clasp. And, whereas I thought the story was buried and forgotten, here it is suddenly raked up again. Why? That's what I want to know."

Hortense was no longer even attempting to fight. He was bringing to bear upon her all his virile strength, all his spite, all his fears, all the threats expressed in his furious gestures and on his features, which were both ridiculous and evil:

"Speak, I want to know. If I have a secret foe, let me defend myself against him! Who is he? Who sent you here? Who urged you to take action? Is it a rival incensed by my good luck, who wants in his turn to benefit by the clasp? Speak, can't you, damn it all. . . or, I swear by Heaven, I'll make you! . . ."

She had an idea that he was reaching out for his revolver and stepped back, holding her arms before her, in the hope of escaping.

They thus struggled against each other; and Hortense, who was becoming more and more frightened, not so much of the attack as of her assailant's distorted face, was beginning to scream, when Pancaldi suddenly stood motionless, with his arms before him, his fingers outstretched and his eyes staring above Hortense's head:

"Who's there? How did you get in?" he asked, in a stifled voice.

Hortense did not even need to turn round to feel assured that Rénine was coming to her assistance and that it was his inexplicable appearance that was causing the dealer such dismay. As a matter of fact, a slender figure stole through a heap of easy chairs and sofas: and Rénine came forward with a tranquil step.

"Who are you?" repeated Pancaldi. "Where do you come from?"

"From up there," he said, very amiably, pointing to the ceiling.

"From up there?"

"Yes, from the first floor. I have been the tenant of the floor above this for the past three months. I heard a noise just now. Some one was calling out for help. So I came down."

"But how did you get in here?"

"By the staircase."

"What staircase?"

"The iron staircase, at the end of the shop. The man who owned it before you had a flat on my floor and used to go up and down by that hidden staircase. You had the door shut off. I opened it."

"But by what right, sir? It amounts to breaking in."

"Breaking in is allowed, when there's a fellow-creature to be rescued."

"Once more, who are you?"

"Prince Rénine. . . and a friend of this lady's," said Rénine, bending over Hortense and kissing her hand.

Pancaldi seemed to be choking, and mumbled:

"Oh, I understand! . . . You instigated the plot. . . it was you who sent the lady. . ."

"It was, M. Pancaldi, it was!"

"And what are your intentions?"

"My intentions are irreproachable. No violence. Simply a little interview. When that is over, you will hand over what I in my turn have come to fetch."

"What?"

"The clasp."

"That, never!" shouted the dealer.

"Don't say no. It's a foregone conclusion."

"No power on earth, sir, can compel me to do such a thing!"

"Shall we send for your wife? Madame Pancaldi will perhaps realize the position better than you do."

The idea of no longer being alone with this unexpected adversary seemed to appeal to Pancaldi. There was a bell on the table beside him. He struck it three times.

"Capital!" exclaimed Rénine "You see, my dear, M. Pancaldi is becoming quite amiable. Not a trace left of the devil broken loose who was going for you just now. No, M. Pancaldi only has to find himself dealing with a man to recover his qualities of courtesy and kindness. A perfect sheep! Which does not mean that things will go quite of themselves. Far from it! There's no more obstinate animal than a sheep. . ."

Right at the end of the shop, between the dealer's writing-desk and the winding staircase, a curtain was raised, admitting a woman who was holding a door open. She might have been thirty years of age. Very simply dressed, she looked, with the apron on her, more like a cook than like the mistress of a household. But she had an attractive face and a pleasing figure.

Hortense, who had followed Rénine, was surprised to recognize her as a maid whom she had had in her service when a girl:

"What! Is that you, Lucienne? Are you Madame Pancaldi?"

The newcomer looked at her, recognized her also and seemed embarrassed. Rénine said to her:

"Your husband and I need your assistance, Madame Pancaldi, to settle a rather complicated matter a matter in which you played an important part. . ."

She came forward without a word, obviously ill at ease, asking her husband, who did not take his eyes off her:

"What is it? . . . What do they want with me? . . . What is he referring to?"

"It's about the clasp!" Pancaldi whispered, under his breath.

These few words were enough to make Madame Pancaldi realize to the full the seriousness of her position. And she did not try to keep her countenance or to retort with futile protests. She sank into a chair, sighing:

"Oh, that's it! . . . I understand. . . Mlle. Hortense has found the track. . . Oh, it's all up with us!"

There was a moment's respite. The struggle between the adversaries had hardly begun, before the husband and wife adopted the attitude of defeated persons whose only hope lay in the victor's clemency. Staring motionless before her, Madame Pancaldi began to cry. Rénine bent over her and said:

"Do you mind if we go over the case from the beginning? We shall then see things more clearly; and I am sure that our interview will lead to a perfectly natural solution. . . This is how things happened: nine years ago, when you were lady's maid to Mlle. Hortense in the country, you made the acquaintance of M. Pancaldi, who soon became your lover. You were both of you Corsicans, in other words, you came from a country where superstitions are very strong and where questions of good and bad luck, the evil eye, and spells and charms exert a profound influence over the lives of one and all. Now it was said that your young mistress' clasp had always brought luck to its owners. That was why, in a weak moment prompted by M. Pancaldi, you stole the clasp. Six months afterwards, you became Madame Pancaldi. . . That is your whole story, is it not, told in a few sentences? The whole story of two people who would have remained honest members of society, if they had been able to resist that casual temptation? . . . I need not tell you how you both succeeded in life and how, possessing the talisman, believing its powers and trusting in yourselves, you rose to the first rank of antiquarians. To-day, well-off, owning this shop, "The Mercury," you attribute the success of your undertakings to that clasp. To lose it would to your eyes spell bankruptcy and poverty. Your whole life has been centred upon it. It is your fetish. It is the little household god who watches over you and guides your steps. It is there, somewhere, hidden in this jungle; and no one of course would ever have suspected anything—for I repeat, you are decent people, but for this one lapse—if an accident had not led me to look into your affairs."

Rénine paused and continued:

"That was two months ago, two months of minute investigations, which presented no difficulty to me, because, having discovered your trail, I hired the flat overhead and was able to use that staircase. . . but, all the same, two months wasted to a certain extent because I have not yet succeeded. And Heaven knows how I have ransacked this shop of yours! There is not a piece of furniture that I have left unsearched, not a plank in the floor that I have not inspected. All to no purpose. Yes, there was one thing, an incidental discovery. In a secret recess in your writing-table, Pancaldi, I turned up a little account-book in which you have set down your remorse, your uneasiness, your fear of punishment and your dread of God's wrath. . . It was highly imprudent of you, Pancaldi! People don't write such confessions! And, above all, they don't leave them lying about! Be this as it may, I read them and I noted one passage, which struck me as particularly important and was of use to me in preparing my plan of campaign: 'Should she come to me, the woman whom I robbed, should she come to me as I saw her in her garden, while Lucienne was taking the clasp; should she appear to me wearing the blue gown and the toque of red leaves, with the jet necklace and the whip of three plaited rushes which she was carrying that day; should she appear to me thus and say: "I have come to claim my property," then I shall understand that her conduct is inspired from on high and that I must obey the decree of Providence.' That is what is written in your book, Pancaldi, and it explains the conduct of the lady whom you call Mlle. Hortense. Acting on my instructions and in accordance with the setting thought out by yourself, she came to you, from the back of beyond, to use your own expression. A little more self-possession on her part; and you know that she would have won the day. Unfortunately, you are a wonderful actor; your sham suicide put her out; and you understood that this was not a decree of Providence, but simply an offensive on the part of your former victim. I had no choice, therefore, but to intervene. Here I am. . . And now let's finish the business. Pancaldi, that clasp!"

"No," said the dealer, who seemed to recover all his energy at the very thought of restoring the clasp.

"And you, Madame Pancaldi."

"I don't know where it is," the wife declared.

"Very well. Then let us come to deeds. Madame Pancaldi, you have a son of seven whom you love with all your heart. This is Thursday and, as on every Thursday, your little boy is to come home alone from his aunt's. Two of my friends are posted on the road by which he returns and, in the absence of instructions to the contrary, will kidnap him as he passes."

Madame Pancaldi lost her head at once:

"My son! Oh, please, please. . . not that! . . . I swear that I know nothing. My husband would never consent to confide in me."

Rénine continued:

"Next point. This evening, I shall lodge an information with the public prosecutor. Evidence: the confessions in the account-book. Consequences: action by the police, search of the premises and the rest."

Pancaldi was silent. The others had a feeling that all these threats did not affect him and that, protected by his fetish, he believed himself to be invulnerable. But his wife fell on her knees at Rénine's feet and stammered:

"No, no. . . I entreat you! . . . It would mean going to prison and I don't want to go! . . . And then my son! . . . Oh, I entreat you! . . ."

Hortense, seized with compassion, took Rénine to one side:

"Poor woman! Let me intercede for her."

"Set your mind at rest," he said. "Nothing is going to happen to her son."

"But your two friends?"

"Sheer bluff."

"Your application to the public prosecutor?"

"A mere threat."

"Then what are you trying to do?"

"To frighten them out of their wits, in the hope of making them drop a remark, a word, which will tell us what we want to know. We've tried every other means. This is the last; and it is a method which, I find, nearly always succeeds. Remember our adventures."

"But if the word which you expect to hear is not spoken?"

"It must be spoken," said Rénine, in a low voice. "We must finish the matter. The hour is at hand."

His eyes met hers; and she blushed crimson at the thought that the hour to which he was alluding was the eighth and that he had no other object than to finish the matter before that eighth hour struck.

"So you see, on the one hand, what you are risking," he said to the Pancaldi pair. "The disappearance of your child. . . and prison: prison for certain, since there is the book with its confessions. And now, on the other hand, here's my offer: twenty thousand francs if you hand over the clasp immediately, this minute. Remember, it isn't worth three louis."

No reply. Madame Pancaldi was crying.

Rénine resumed, pausing between each proposal:

"I'll double my offer. . . I'll treble it. . . Hang it all, Pancaldi, you're unreasonable! . . . I suppose you want me to make it a round sum? All right: a hundred thousand francs."

He held out his hand as if there was no doubt that they would give him the clasp.

Madame Pancaldi was the first to yield and did so with a sudden outburst of rage against her husband:

"Well, confess, can't you? . . . Speak up! . . . Where have you hidden it? . . . Look here, you aren't going to be obstinate, what? If you are, it means ruin. . . and poverty. . . And then there's our boy! . . . Speak out, do!"

Hortense whispered:

"Rénine, this is madness; the clasp has no value. . ."

"Never fear," said Rénine, "he's not going to accept. . . But look at him. . . How excited he is! Exactly what I wanted. . . Ah, this, you know, is really exciting! . . . To make people lose their heads! To rob them of all control over what they are thinking and saying! . . . And, in the midst of this confusion, in the storm that tosses them to and fro, to catch sight of the tiny spark which will flash forth somewhere or other! . . . Look at him! Look at the fellow! A hundred thousand francs for a valueless pebble. . . if not, prison: it's enough to turn any man's head!"

Pancaldi, in fact, was grey in the face; his lips were trembling and a drop of saliva was trickling from their corners. It was easy to guess the seething turmoil of his whole being, shaken by conflicting emotions, by the clash between greed and fear. Suddenly he burst out; and it was obvious that his words were pouring forth at random, without his knowing in the least what he was saying:

"A hundred thousand francs! Two hundred thousand! Five hundred thousand! A million! A two fig for your millions! What's the use of millions? One loses them. They disappear. . . They go. . . There's only one thing that counts: luck. It's on your side or else against you. And luck has been on my side these last nine years. It has never betrayed me; and you expect me to betray it? Why? Out of fear? Prison? My son? Bosh! . . . No harm will come to me so long as I compel luck to work on my behalf. It's my servant, it's my friend. It clings to the clasp. How? How can I tell? It's the cornelian, no doubt. . . There are magic stones, which hold happiness, as others hold fire, or sulphur, or gold. . ."

Rénine kept his eyes fixed upon him, watching for the least word, the least modulation of the voice. The curiosity-dealer was now laughing, with a nervous laugh, while resuming the self-control of a man who feels sure of himself: and he walked up to Rénine with jerky movements that revealed an increasing resolution:

"Millions? My dear sir, I wouldn't have them as a gift. The little bit of stone which I possess is worth much more than that. And the proof of it lies in all the pains which you are at to take it from me. Aha! Months devoted to looking for it, as you yourself confess! Months in which you turned everything topsy-turvy, while I, who suspected nothing, did not even defend myself! Why should I? The little thing defended itself all alone. . . It does not want to be discovered and it sha'n't be. . . It likes being here. . . It presides over a good, honest business that satisfies it. . . Pancaldi's luck! Why, it's known to all the neighbourhood, among all the dealers! I proclaim it from the house-tops: 'I'm a lucky man!' I even made so bold as to take the god of luck, Mercury, as my patron! He too protects me. See, I've got Mercuries all over my shop! Look up there, on that shelf, a whole row of statuettes, like the one over the front-door, proofs signed by a great sculptor who went smash and sold them to me. . . Would you like one, my dear sir? It will bring you luck too. Take your pick! A present from Pancaldi, to make up to you for your defeat! Does that suit you?"

He put a stool against the wall, under the shelf, took down a statuette and plumped it into Rénine's arms. And, laughing heartily, growing more and more excited as his enemy seemed to yield ground and to fall back before his spirited attack, he explained:

"Well done! He accepts! And the fact that he accepts shows that we are all agreed! Madame Pancaldi, don't distress yourself. Your son's coming back and nobody's going to prison! Good-bye, Mlle. Hortense! Good-day, sir! Hope to see you again! If you want to speak to me at any time, just give three thumps on the ceiling. Good-bye. . . don't forget your present. . . and may Mercury be kind to you! Good-bye, my dear Prince! Good-bye, Mlle. Hortense! . . ."

He hustled them to the iron staircase, gripped each of them by the arm in turn and pushed them up to the little door hidden at the top of the stairs.

And the strange thing was that Rénine made no protest. He did not attempt to resist. He allowed himself to be led along like a naughty child that is taken up to bed.

Less than five minutes had elapsed between the moment when he made his offer to Pancaldi and the moment when Pancaldi turned him out of the shop with a statuette in his arms.

THE DINING-ROOM AND DRAWING-ROOM OF the flat which Rénine had taken on the first floor looked out upon the street. The table in the dining-room was laid for two.

"Forgive me, won't you?" said Rénine, as he opened the door of the drawing-room for Hortense. "I thought that, whatever happened, I

　　　　　MAURICE LEBLANC

should most likely see you this evening and that we might as well dine together. Don't refuse me this kindness, which will be the last favour granted in our last adventure."

Hortense did not refuse him. The manner in which the battle had ended was so different from everything that she had seen hitherto that she felt disconcerted. At any rate, why should she refuse, seeing that the terms of the contract had not been fulfilled?

Rénine left the room to give an order to his manservant. Two minutes later, he came back for Hortense. It was then a little past seven.

There were flowers on the table; and the statue of Mercury, Pancaldi's present, stood overtopping them.

"May the god of luck preside over our repast," said Rénine.

He was full of animation and expressed his great delight at having her sitting opposite him:

"Yes," he exclaimed, "I had to resort to powerful means and attract you by the bait of the most fabulous enterprises. You must confess that my letter was jolly smart! The three rushes, the blue gown; simply irresistible! And, when I had thrown in a few puzzles of my own invention, such as the seventy-five beads of the necklace and the old woman with the silver rosary, I knew that you were bound to succumb to the temptation. Don't be angry with me. I wanted to see you and I wanted it to be today. You have come and I thank you."

He next told her how he had got on the track of the stolen trinket:

"You hoped, didn't you, in laying down that condition, that I shouldn't be able to fulfil it? You made a mistake, my dear. The test, at least at the beginning, was easy enough, because it was based upon an undoubted fact: the talismanic character attributed to the clasp. I had only to hunt about and see whether among the people around you, among your servants, there was ever any one upon whom that character may have exercised some attraction. Now, on the list of persons which I succeeded in drawing up. I at once noticed the name of Mlle. Lucienne, as coming from Corsica. This was my starting-point. The rest was a mere concatenation of events."

Hortense stared at him in amazement. How was it that he was accepting his defeat with such a careless air and even talking in a tone of triumph, whereas really he had been soundly beaten by Pancaldi and even made to look just a trifle ridiculous?

She could not help letting him feel this; and the fashion in which she did so betrayed a certain disappointment, a certain humiliation:

"Everything is a concatenation of events: very well. But the chain is broken, because, when all is said, though you know the thief, you did not succeed in laying hands upon the stolen clasp."

The reproach was obvious. Rénine had not accustomed her to failure. And furthermore she was irritated to see how heedlessly he was accepting a blow which, after all, entailed the ruin of any hopes that he might have entertained.

He did not reply. He had filled their two glasses with champagne and was slowly emptying his own, with his eyes fixed on the statuette of Mercury. He turned it about on its pedestal and examined it with the eye of a delighted connoisseur:

"What a beautiful thing is a harmonious line! Colour does not uplift me so much as outline, proportion, symmetry and all the wonderful properties of form. Look at this little statue. Pancaldi's right: it's the work of a great artist. The legs are both slender and muscular; the whole figure gives an impression of buoyancy and speed. It is very well done. There's only one fault, a very slight one: perhaps you've not noticed it?"

"Yes, I have," said Hortense. "It struck me the moment I saw the sign, outside. You mean, don't you, a certain lack of balance? The god is leaning over too far on the leg that carries him. He looks as though he were going to pitch forward."

"That's very clever of you," said Rénine. "The fault is almost imperceptible and it needs a trained eye to see it. Really, however, as a matter of logic, the weight of the body ought to have its way and, in accordance with natural laws, the little god ought to take a header."

After a pause he continued:

"I noticed that flaw on the first day. How was it that I did not draw an inference at once? I was shocked because the artist had sinned against an aesthetic law, whereas I ought to have been shocked because he had overlooked a physical law. As though art and nature were not blended together! And as though the laws of gravity could be disturbed without some fundamental reason!"

"What do you mean?" asked Hortense, puzzled by these reflections, which seemed so far removed from their secret thoughts. "What do you mean?"

"Oh, nothing!" he said. "I am only surprised that I didn't understand sooner why Mercury did not plump forward, as he should have done."

"And what is the reason?"

"The reason? I imagine that Pancaldi, when pulling the statuette about to make it serve his purpose, must have disturbed its balance, but that this balance was restored by something which holds the little god back and which makes up for his really too dangerous posture."

"Something, you say?"

"Yes, a counterweight."

Hortense gave a start. She too was beginning to see a little light. She murmured:

"A counterweight? . . . Are you thinking that it might be. . . in the pedestal?"

"Why not?"

"Is that possible? But, if so, how did Pancaldi come to give you this statuette?"

"He never gave me *this* one," Rénine declared. "I took this one myself."

"But where? And when?"

"Just now, while you were in the drawing-room. I got out of that window, which is just over the signboard and beside the niche containing the little god. And I exchanged the two, that is to say, I took the statue which was outside and put the one which Pancaldi gave me in its place."

"But doesn't that one lean forward?"

"No, no more than the others do, on the shelf in his shop. But Pancaldi is not an artist. A lack of equilibrium does not impress him; he will see nothing wrong; and he will continue to think himself favoured by luck, which is another way of saying that luck will continue to favour him. Meanwhile, here's the statuette, the one used for the sign. Am I to break the pedestal and take your clasp out of the leaden sheath, soldered to the back of the pedestal, which keeps Mercury steady?"

"No, no, there's no need for that," Hortense hurriedly murmured.

Rénine's intuition, his subtlety, the skill with which he had managed the whole business: to her, for the moment, all these things remained in the background. But she suddenly remembered that the eighth adventure was completed, that Rénine had surmounted every obstacle, that the test had turned to his advantage and that the extreme limit of time fixed for the last of the adventures was not yet reached.

He had the cruelty to call attention to the fact:

"A quarter to eight," he said.

An oppressive silence fell between them. Both felt its discomfort to such a degree that they hesitated to make the least movement. In order to break it, Rénine jested:

"That worthy M. Pancaldi, how good it was of him to tell me what I wished to know! I knew, however, that by exasperating him, I should end by picking up the missing clue in what he said. It was just as though one were to hand some one a flint and steel and suggest to him that he was to use it. In the end, the spark is obtained. In my case, what produced the spark was the unconscious but inevitable comparison which he drew between the cornelian clasp, the element of luck, and Mercury, the god of luck. That was enough. I understood that this association of ideas arose from his having actually associated the two factors of luck by embodying one in the other, or, to speak more plainly, by hiding the trinket in the statuette. And I at once remembered the Mercury outside the door and its defective poise. . ."

Rénine suddenly interrupted himself. It seemed to him that all his remarks were falling on deaf ears. Hortense had put her hand to her forehead and, thus veiling her eyes, sat motionless and remote.

She was indeed not listening. The end of this particular adventure and the manner in which Rénine had acted on this occasion no longer interested her. What she was thinking of was the complex series of adventures amid which she had been living for the past three months and the wonderful behaviour of the man who had offered her his devotion. She saw, as in a magic picture, the fabulous deeds performed by him, all the good that he had done, the lives saved, the sorrows assuaged, the order restored wherever his masterly will had been brought to bear. Nothing was impossible to him. What he undertook to do he did. Every aim that he set before him was attained in advance. And all this without excessive effort, with the calmness of one who knows his own strength and knows that nothing can resist it.

Then what could she do against him? Why should she defend herself and how? If he demanded that she should yield, would he not know how to make her do so and would this last adventure be any more difficult for him than the others? Supposing that she ran away: did the wide world contain a retreat in which she would be safe from his pursuit? From the first moment of their first meeting, the end was certain, since Rénine had decreed that it should be so.

However, she still cast about for weapons, for protection of some sort; and she said to herself that, though he had fulfilled the eight conditions and restored the cornelian clasp to her before the eighth hour had struck, she was nevertheless protected by the fact that this eighth hour was to strike on the clock of the Château de Halingre and not elsewhere. It was a formal compact. Rénine had said that day, gazing on the lips which he longed to kiss:

"The old brass pendulum will start swinging again; and, when, on the fixed date, the clock once more strikes eight, then. . ."

She looked up. He was not moving either, but sat solemnly, patiently waiting.

She was on the point of saying, she was even preparing her words:

"You know, our agreement says it must be the Halingre clock. All the other conditions have been fulfilled. . . but not this one. So I am free, am I not? I am entitled not to keep my promise, which, moreover, I never made, but which in any case falls to the ground? . . . And I am perfectly free. . . released from any scruple of conscience? . . ."

She had not time to speak. At that precise moment, there was a click behind her, like that of a clock about to strike.

A first stroke sounded, then a second, then a third.

Hortense moaned. She had recognized the very sound of the old clock, the Halingre clock, which three months ago, by breaking in a supernatural manner the silence of the deserted château, had set both of them on the road of the eight adventures.

She counted the strokes. The clock struck eight.

"Ah!" she murmured, half swooning and hiding her face in her hands. "The clock. . . the clock is here. . . the one from over there. . . I recognize its voice. . ."

She said no more. She felt that Rénine had his eyes fixed upon her and this sapped all her energies. Besides, had she been able to recover them, she would have been no better off nor sought to offer him the least resistance, for the reason that she did not wish to resist. All the adventures were over, but one remained to be undertaken, the anticipation of which wiped out the memory of all the rest. It was the adventure of love, the most delightful, the most bewildering, the most adorable of all adventures. She accepted fate's decree, rejoicing in all that might come, because she was in love. She smiled in spite of herself, as she reflected that happiness was again to enter her life at the very moment when her well-beloved was bringing her the cornelian clasp.

The clock struck the hour for the second time.

Hortense raised her eyes to Rénine. She struggled a few seconds longer. But she was like a charmed bird, incapable of any movement of revolt; and at the eighth stroke she fell upon his breast and offered him her lips. . .

THE END

A Note About the Author

Maurice Leblanc (1864–1941) was a French novelist and short story writer. Born and raised in Rouen, Normandy, Leblanc attended law school before dropping out to pursue a writing career in Paris. There, he made a name for himself as a leading author of crime fiction, publishing critically acclaimed stories and novels with moderate commercial success. On July 15th, 1905, Leblanc published a story in *Je sais tout*, a popular French magazine, featuring Arsène Lupin, gentleman thief. The character, inspired by Sir Arthur Conan Doyle's Sherlock Holmes stories, brought Leblanc both fame and fortune, featuring in 21 novels and short story collections and defining his career as one of the bestselling authors of the twentieth century. Appointed to the *Légion d'Honneur*, France's highest order of merit, Leblanc and his works remain cultural touchstones for generations of devoted readers. His stories have inspired numerous adaptations, including *Lupin,* a smash-hit 2021 television series.

A Note from the Publisher

Spanning many genres, from non-fiction essays to literature classics to children's books and lyric poetry, Mint Edition books showcase the master works of our time in a modern new package. The text is freshly typeset, is clean and easy to read, and features a new note about the author in each volume. Many books also include exclusive new introductory material. Every book boasts a striking new cover, which makes it as appropriate for collecting as it is for gift giving. Mint Edition books are only printed when a reader orders them, so natural resources are not wasted. We're proud that our books are never manufactured in excess and exist only in the exact quantity they need to be read and enjoyed.

bookfinity™

Discover more of your favorite classics with Bookfinity™.

- Track your reading with custom book lists.
- Get great book recommendations for your personalized Reader Type.
- Add reviews for your favorite books.
- AND MUCH MORE!

Visit **bookfinity.com** and take the fun Reader Type quiz to get started.

Enjoy our classic and modern companion pairings!

Classic & Modern

9 781513 292427